MW00917573

Trailer
ON THE FLY

BOOK TWO OF THE TIME TRAVEL TRAILER

Karen Musser Nortman

COVER DESIGN BY WICKED BOOK COVERS

Dedicated to all of us who think if we could just have do-overs, everything would be great.

TABLE OF CONTENTS

CHAPTER 1

"I NEED A vacation. I don't care where." The woman sat in the client chair and fiddled with her purse. I looked at her face and wondered at the cause of her nervousness. It was pretty unusual to get such an open request.

"Um, are you thinking something like a group tour or a cruise? Or something on your own?

"Not on my own," she said firmly.

I thought about some of the tours I had pending that still had openings. "We have a bus tour coming up in June to the Black Hills and Yellowstone."

"No." She was even more definite. "What about a city? Don't you have any Chicago or New York tours? Something like that?"

"Sure." I pulled out a couple of brochures and spread them in front of her. "Here's one also to Charleston, South Carolina and Savannah, Georgia. Did you have a particular time in mind?"

She sighed. "Not really. The sooner, the better, I guess."

I was a little baffled. Usually clients come into my travel agency excited and fired up. They each have their own dreams of the ideal trip. This woman seemed at best resigned about the prospect of having to take a vacation.

I turned to my computer. "Let me get some specifics in here. Would you give me your name and phone number?" I tried to be upbeat but it wasn't easy.

"Naomi Burks." She proceeded in a monotone with her phone number and address.

I hadn't introduced myself. She probably saw my name on the office door, but still... "I'm Lynne McBriar. Good to meet you."

She didn't look particularly interested so I asked her for open dates, preferences and interests. "Will you be alone or traveling with a companion?"

"Alone, definitely. And I don't want any wilderness stuff, just something busy that will keep my mind off of things."

Curiouser and curiouser. I checked the clock on the wall behind her. Almost noon.

"Look," I said, "do you have time for lunch? I feel like I need to know you a little better to get an idea of what would be best suited to your needs."

"Don't you have something I could sign up for now?"

"We do. And I can do that for you. But, if you aren't busy for lunch, it would give us a chance to chat about the possibilities."

Something wasn't right here. Even though she seemed open to a multitude of possibilities, I had the feeling that the actual choice might be fraught with pitfalls for her.

"I suppose I have to eat," she said.

Okay, she's excited now, right?

"How about we grab a sandwich at The Frog—my treat—and we can talk while we eat?"

She agreed with the same resignation she had displayed toward a trip, so I grabbed my jacket and purse before she could change her mind.

The Frog sounds like it might be a trendy, fun cafe but it's really just a plain local diner, not old enough, upscale enough, or funky enough to be a happenin' place. Just a diner. The food is fresh and the place is clean. End of story.

When we walked in, Sandra, the owner, cook, cashier, and waitress, said, "Hi, Lynne. Good to see you." She gave Naomi a pleasant smile, but showed no recognition. "Have a seat anywhere."

We took a table by the window. I ordered a tuna salad sandwich on rye and Naomi did the same. I had the feeling she would have copied me no matter what I chose.

3

As we sipped our iced tea, while I tried to think how to elicit the actual type of trip she had in mind, she burst out with, "My doctor thinks this would be good for me."

"You have health issues? Anything I should be aware of in planning your trip?"

She shook her head. "Not physically. I'm fine." She used her straw to stir her tea and stared out the window.

"I'm not trying to be nosy, but I get the feeling that you need something very specific and I don't want to sell you something that is not going to meet any of those needs."

She looked back at me, her eyes a watery light blue and I realized how thin she was and how sallow her skin was. She could be quite pretty, as my mother would say, with a little weight on those cheeks and a little color.

When she said nothing, I tried a different tack.

"Naomi, do you work?"

"Part time, at Little Feet. But don't worry, I can pay for this."

Little Feet was a local day care facility and well-known for good child care and low wages. The way she twisted everything I said, she must be in a very dark place.

"I'm sorry—I didn't mean that. I'm only wondering what your situation is as far as time off, notice required, that kind of thing. Do you want to tell me what kind of vacation your doctor thinks you need?"

Sandra brought our sandwiches, asked if we needed

anything else, and left us to our privacy.

"No—oh, what the hell. I suffer from depression," she said, took a bite of her sandwich, and wiped her mouth primly after.

I waited, chewing my own sandwich.

She swallowed. "It's been about ten years. I lost a very good friend. A woman I grew up with. We were neighbors and both only children. Almost like sisters." She took another bite.

I nodded. "I'm an only child, too. It does make those friendships really important." Still I thought, ten years is a long time to nurse grief and put the rest of your life aside. I felt very sorry for her. As trite and stupid as it sounded, I said, "I'm sorry for your loss."

"It was at a camping event," she said. "That's why I don't want to go to any wilderness areas. I want plenty of people around."

"What happened?"

"It was a Sisters on the Fly event. Part of our campground got hit with a flash flood. Beverly was washed away and was never found." Her voice broke.

"And then what?"

"Nothing. They never found her. If I only knew—," she put her sandwich down and covered her face with her hands.

I was beginning to grasp the cause of her paralysis. "Where did this happen??

"You know about Sisters on the Fly?"

I nodded. I had heard about their wilderness adventures and other gatherings from travel industry journals and conventions. Started by two sisters, they organized outdoor events exclusively for women, including fly fishing, camping, kayaking, and horseback riding.

"Bev and I talked each other into joining. We had a great time. Some amazing women in that group." She smiled slightly and shook her head, remembering. "We went on a kayaking weekend in southern Missouri—at Paulie's Shoots State Park. The campground was right by the river."

"But—," I paused, confused. "Wasn't there an investigation?"

"Oh, yeah. County sheriff and state investigators and everything. They never found her." Tears began to form in her eyes.

"I am so sorry. You do need to get away. Let's talk about things like climate, stuff you would like to see or do, and I promise I will find you the perfect vacation."

I steered her away from her friend's disappearance and finally got some information that I could use. She expressed a slight interest in the Charleston-Savannah tour and decided to go ahead with that.

Sandra returned to offer dessert, which we both declined, and she wrote out the check.

"How's Dinah doing?"

"Fine," I said. "I don't remember my sophomore year

being as busy as my daughter's."

Sandra shook her head and smiled. "They grow up too fast."

I agreed and Naomi and I walked back to my office. I promised to be in touch with updates for her tour and she disappeared down the street.

CHAPTER 2

THE NEXT WEEKEND I was thinking again about Naomi and her friend Bev. After an afternoon of working in the garden, I took my laptop out to my screen porch and searched for flash floods in Missouri in 2005. There weren't many and I soon discovered an item about a Beverly Borcherd who went missing just as Naomi had described. There wasn't much information in the original item—as Naomi had said, Bev was believed to have been washed away in the flood and was never found.

As I sat thinking about it, my gaze fell on the spot behind my garage where last year I kept the old 1937 camper trailer I had bought from my friend Ben Walker. I still owned it, but now it was back behind Ben's barn, locked up and surrounded by weeds.

It was a great piece of the past, with a wood interior and checked linoleum floor. The cabinets all had refrigerator-style latches and the icebox was an old wooden style that required a block of ice in the top. It worked quite well for short trips. I had stripped the Sixties wallpaper and refinished all of the wood. I made curtains out of vintage aprons and scrounged thrift shops for period accessories. It was sweet.

It also time traveled.

"Hey, Mom, what's up?" Dinah had walked out on the porch.

"Not much."

She glanced at my computer screen. "What are you looking up?"

"Oh, an old missing person case in Missouri."

She frowned at me. "Why?"

I explained about Naomi and her friend.

"So are you going to go back in the camper and find out what happened to her?"

"What?"

"Sure." Dinah looked out at the spot I had been staring at. "Isn't that what you're thinking?"

I was taken aback. I hadn't consciously thought about it, but maybe she knew me better than I did.

"I don't think that would work. We couldn't control what date it went to," I said.

She used both hands to pull her blond hair into a pile on top of her head—sort of a messy Gibson Girl. "Get some stuff from Just Junk from that year."

"I don't know—seemed like it needed to be attached to the trailer—flooring, wallpaper, like that."

The year before, I bought the trailer and each time I took another layer of remodeling efforts off the inside, Dinah and I were transported back to the era of the previous remodel. I know—far-fetched, but we were there.

She shrugged. "Maybe some carpet from that year? Put it in temporarily."

"I took it back to Ben's because I thought we didn't want any more 'trips.' There are too many questions. For instance, last year we always went back to a time before either of us were born. So there wasn't a duplicate of either of us wandering around. I don't know what would happen if I only went back ten years."

"I'd be five. I was really cute then," Dinah grinned, then grew serious. "Maybe you're right. In a lot of the time travel books, if you run into yourself at a different age and change the course of events, you can cause a time line to split."

"You're still cute, just more obnoxious. But there's a bigger problem."

"Bigger than a time line split?"

She had devoured time travel novels after our experience, and, I'm afraid, took them as scientific truth.

"Okay, a more *immediate* problem. The campground was hit by a flash flood. If I took the trailer back to that place at that time, how would I avoid being washed away myself? And if I warned everyone, how would I explain that? And why would they believe me?"

"Hmmm. We need to think about this." She flopped in the bamboo papasan chair, squirmed around until her hair hung over the front and her feet and legs over the back. Apparently, this would help her think.

I shook my head. "I don't see any way for it to work. And even if it did, should I go back to prevent everything bad that has ever happened to everyone we know? What would *that* do to the time line — and the present?"

"Right," she said. Still thinking. "What if you went back and observed and didn't do anything? You could tell your client what happened to her friend and that might help her."

"I could and it might. But how could I stand back and not try to prevent her death? And how could I explain what I knew?"

She sat upright again, bounced up out of the chair, and shrugged her shoulders. "I don't know, Mom. You'd better think about it more before you do anything. I'm going over to Tish's house to study for our lit test." And she was gone, blissfully oblivious that she had brought up the conundrum in the first place.

Disturbed, I stared at my laptop screen. I looked for anything related to Beverly Borcherd's drowning. An article from two weeks after the flood mentioned that Beverly and one other person had not been found. The search was called off.

Several entries were the usual come-ons to obtain police and other records for a fee or to find out if Beverly was part of your family tree. A listing at LinkedIn had very little information except that she was the CEO of a pharmaceutical consulting firm and held a PhD in chemistry. There were no 'skills' checked by other LinkedIn members.

The next item that came up in the search was from 2002. A New Jersey newspaper article identified Beverly Borcherd as a whistle blower, accusing Bailoff Labs of falsifying drug trials. Interesting.

According to her LinkedIn profile, the consulting firm was founded in 2003. Maybe she formed the business because she lost her job over the whistle blowing? The profile didn't list any employment previous to 2003, but in the whistle blowing article, she was described as a Bailoff employee.

I told myself this was all pointless for the reasons I had given Dinah. However, my curiosity was piqued and I did a search on Naomi Burks. There was nothing—no LinkedIn or Facebook pages. I was scrolling down the references when I hear the side door open.

"Lynne?" It was my husband, Kurt. We were currently separated, going through counseling, and making some progress. I didn't usually see him on the weekend unless he was picking up Dinah.

"On the porch," I yelled back.

"Hey." He came in and gently squeezed my shoulder. We both were still a little uncomfortable with spontaneous displays of affection. He sat in one of the other swivel chairs at the table.

"Hey, yourself. What's up?"

"Is Dinah around?"

"No, she went over to Tish's to 'study.'"

He laughed and straightened his glasses—a recent addition that I still was getting used to. "Right. Well, I thought if my two favorite girls weren't busy tonight, I'd take you out to supper and to a movie. Sort of a date night."

I grinned. "When we were dating, we didn't have a fifteen-year-old tagging along."

"True, but she's part of the package now."

"I'm available. All of my other dates cancelled out."

Kurt pulled out his phone. "My lucky break. I'll see if I can be so fortunate with Dinah." He dialed our daughter and I could hear her squeals of delight from where I sat. She was definitely a daddy's girl. He covered the mouthpiece with his hand. "5:30 okay?"

I looked at my watch. Almost 5:00. "Yeah, I can make that. I'd better jump in the shower now, though." I left him catching up with Dinah and went to get the leaves and grass out of my hair.

AFTER WE PICKED UP Dinah, we debated between burgers and Mexican and ended up at the local Italian place. Kurt and I both ordered the eggplant parmesan special with veal and salad with house dressing and Dinah got her usual spaghetti with nothing except meatballs. Dinah would order spaghetti in the fanciest restaurant in Paris.

The waitress brought a basket of breadsticks and dipping sauce. Dinah picked up her breadstick and gestured toward Kurt with it. "Mom tell you she's thinking about time traveling again?"

Kurt almost choked on his bite of arugula. He had been a part of our final trip the previous summer, so it wasn't the idea of time travel that shocked him; rather that it might happen again. He looked around quickly to make sure no one was listening, glared at me, and said in a stage whisper, "What are you thinking?"

I targeted Dinah with my own fierce stare. "Dinah. That's not true." I looked back at Kurt. "That was her suggestion." As soon as I said it, I realized I sounded like a seven-year-old tattletale.

I took a deep breath. "Let me explain." I told him about Naomi Burks. "I was looking up what had happened to her friend when Dinah came by. She suggested using the trailer to go back to see what happened, but we discussed all of the problems associated with that. I mean, how could you not try to save the friend if you could? And what would that do to the future? I mean, the present?"

Kurt relaxed and nodded as he chewed his salad and considered.

"What I don't understand," Dinah said, twirling a second breadstick between her fingers, "is why what happened last summer didn't screw up the timeline. How was Ben able to take Minnie back and leave her? What happened to the other Minnie? And how did she go back to the age she was at that time, before her accident?"

"Good questions. I've told Ben about our adventures last summer but he's never really explained that."

The waitress brought our meals and we occupied ourselves with the business of eating for the next few minutes.

"So, to be clear," Kurt said to me, "you're *not* seriously thinking about going back and rescuing the woman."

"No, I am not. I'm just curious about this client and how ten years later she is still so overcome with grief that she almost seems—like a zombie, or something."

"She obviously was very close to this friend," Kurt said.

"Of course. I'm not belittling it. But she's paralyzed by it."

"Does she have a job?" Dinah asked.

"Yes, she works at Little Feet. I don't know for how long—I get the impression she hasn't lived in town very long. I've never heard her name before."

"Can I go back to Tish's when we get done? We were going to watch a movie." Dinah mopped up spaghetti sauce with yet another breadstick.

Kurt sighed. "I thought maybe we'd all take in a movie."

"Aw, Dad, we already rented one. I'm sorry."

"What happened to studying for your test?" He grinned and patted her hand. "We'll do it another time."

"Not overnight though," I said. "I'll pick you up at Tish's—about 10:00?"

"Sure."

WE DROPPED DINAH off and when we got back to my house, Kurt put his truck in park and said, "Got time for a nightcap?"

I smiled and, on impulse, leaned over and kissed his cheek. "Of course."

With the familiarity born of living in this house for fifteen years, Kurt poured me a glass of white wine and fixed himself a Manhattan. He wiped up the counter and we headed to the screen porch, seating ourselves in the comfy Adirondack chairs.

He leaned back in his chair. "Dinah said she's applied to a job at the pool for the summer?"

"Yeah, at the concession stand. I think it'll be good for her, don't you?"

He nodded. "Definitely. A little responsibility certainly won't hurt—as long as she doesn't talk everyone to death. Or spend all of her time on her phone."

"She says she has to turn her phone in at the beginning of each shift. What are you working on these days?" I asked. Kurt was a programming whiz and had recently gone on his own to develop video games and apps. It had been a dream of his for years, and our marriage counselor, Scott Waghorn, had encouraged him to try it. He was a much happier person.

He set down his drink and leaned forward. "I'm glad you asked. It's really interesting. There's been a move in recent years to create games to help people deal with depression and emotional stress. They're used especially with teenagers, but now there's a call for games that are appropriate with senior citizens. I have a contract to do that. It requires a lot of background reading, and I'm working with a psychologist, and I'm finding it fascinating."

I was seriously impressed. "Wow. That would be amazing. But can you get seniors to use them?"

"More of them are computer literate than you realize. Think of your mom."

"You're right. She does email, Facebook, and downloads ebooks, I guess. Is that enough skill to play a video game?"

"It's enough to *learn* how to play one. These games have the added advantage of helping older folks keep their minds active."

I sat thinking about Naomi Burks and her depression. "Do the games have to be designed for depression in order to be helpful?"

"No, actually, some studies show that the thought processes help. I think that's how you would say it. Why?"

I pulled my feet up under me. "I keep thinking about my client, Naomi. Like I said, she seems to have completely given up on life. I wonder if something like that could help her."

"Maybe, but it would be better if she did it with the supervision of a therapist." He swirled the ice cubes in his glass and then looked at me. "So you really are not thinking of using that trailer to try and change things?" I might have resented his attempt at control, except I could see the concern on his face.

"No, I'm not. Like I said, there are an awful lot of questions about time travel that even the internet doesn't have the answers for." I smiled.

CHAPTER 3

A FEW DAYS later, I put together a folder with Naomi Burks' tour information and tickets, tied it up with a cute map-printed ribbon, and slipped a small box of chocolates under the bow. Sometimes I'm so clever, I can hardly stand it.

I called the Little Feet Daycare Center.

"Little Feet," a cheery young voice said.

"Hi. I'd like to talk to Naomi Burks."

"Oh! I don't think she's here today. Let me check." Some really obnoxious hold music came on, loud and distorted. They must sell bad recordings especially for that. Fortunately, the receptionist was back quickly.

"Nope. She called in sick today. Can I take a message or have someone else help you?"

"No, that's okay. Thank you." I hung up.

I had noticed that Naomi lived on my way home so right before I locked up, I dialed her number. The voice mail picked up immediately. It was the robo-voice that is the default for voice mail—not Naomi. I declined to leave a message and hung up. I decided to stop by there anyway; she might be on the phone, causing the voicemail to pick up.

Her home was a small green ranch in need of paint. Neglected gardens along the front sprouted more weeds than flowers. The yard had been mowed, but there were no personal touches. The place looked as sad as Naomi had.

The inside front door was standing open. I didn't see a doorbell so I knocked on the screen. I was sure she wouldn't have left the door open if she was gone, so when there was no answer, I called through the door.

"Naomi? It's Lynne McBriar, from the travel agency."

Still no answer. I looked around the entrance. The rusty mailbox hung crooked alongside the door and was overflowing with catalogs and what appeared to be junk mail. Odd that she hadn't brought it in if she was home.

I walked around the side of the house and noticed a small detached garage at the back of the lot. The garage door was open and an old rusted gray Honda presented its backside to the street. I was becoming very concerned. I had only met this woman once, but her overwhelming despondency at the time overcame my reluctance to walk into someone else's house unbidden.

I returned to the front entrance and tried the screen door. It opened with a creaky protest. The tiny living room was sparsely furnished with what appeared to be high quality pieces. A small flat-screen TV perched on an antique walnut table with a marble top. I didn't see anything personal; no magazines, books or photos. No art work; not even any throw pillows or accessories of any kind.

"Naomi?" I called out again. "It's Lynne McBriar."

The kitchen was through a door at the back of the living room. It could have been used in a Seventies sitcom with only the addition of some harvest gold and orange accessories. A few dishes were stacked in the sink.

Another door led to a hallway. I walked along, calling out "Hello?" a couple more times. The first door opened on a small bedroom, furnished only with several sealed packing boxes. Next was a bath, again with only the bare necessities — a single set of towels and a lonely toothbrush poking out of a plastic tumbler.

The door at the end of the hall was partially closed. Through the opening, I could see the end of the bed with a jeans-clad leg half off the bed. My throat closed up as I pushed at the door.

"Naomi?" I had a sudden thought that she was going to sit up and ask me what I was doing in her house. She may not even remember me. But I was willing to swallow the embarrassment if she was okay.

No such luck.

She didn't move. I rushed in and shook her arm, calling her name. Then I saw the brown plastic bottle by her left hand, the lid laying several inches away. It was empty and the label said Prozac.

My hand was shaking so badly I could barely punch 911 into my phone. Perhaps that's why they make the emergency number so short. While it rang, I felt for a pulse with my left hand. I thought there was a very faint beat but couldn't be sure. It was hard to tell over my own pounding heart.

"What is your emergency?"

"I want to report, I mean—I need an ambulance. I think a woman has overdosed on pills."

"What is your address, ma'am?"

"Um—it's not my house—Storm Street, I think. I can't remember the number!" I rushed out of the room back to the front door. "I'm checking now! Just a minute."

"Please stay calm, ma'am if you can. Is the woman conscious?"

"No!" I reached the door and stepped outside looking for a house number. It was above the door. "801! The number is 801."

I hurried back in, catching my toe on the door sill and nearly falling. I yelped and the operator said, "Are you all right, ma'am?"

"Yes, yes. I just tripped. What do you need to know? She's unconscious—I think there may be a faint pulse.

There's an empty bottle of Prozac beside her on the bed."

"Okay, that's good. I have personnel on the way. Please stay on the line."

"I will." I returned to the bedroom and felt her forehead. "She feels kind of cold and clammy."

"Okay, when the ambulance gets there, give them the pill bottle. Okay?"

"Sure. When will they be here?"

"Soon. Do you know the woman's name?"

"Naomi Burks." I spelled it.

"Are you a relative?"

"No. I'm her travel agent. I stopped to leave her some information for a trip. I only met her once."

"What is your name?"

By the time I had given her my information, I could hear the siren. I rushed back outside to flag them down.

I FOLLOWED THE AMBULANCE to the hospital in nearby Black Hawk. I was still shaking and when I reached the parking lot, sat for a moment to gather myself. Before I went into the ER, I called Dinah and explained what had happened.

"Oh, Mom—how awful. Good thing you stopped there." She tried to sound casual, but I could tell she too was shaken by the news.

"Yes. It will probably be a while before I get home. There's some leftover ham in the refrigerator. Do you have anything on tonight?"

"No, I have to study for my biology test tomorrow."

"Okay, I should be home in a couple of hours. If it's going to be later, I'll call."

"Take care, Mom."

Inside, I went to the desk and explained my connection to Naomi Burks.

The receptionist, an older woman with "Iris" on her name tag, looked at her forms. "Do you have any information on her family?"

"I don't. She's a client of mine and I found her by accident. I really don't know much about her."

"Do you know the names of any friends we could call?"

"No. But she works at Little Feet — the day care center — and I know the owner. Should I check with her?"

"Give me her name and phone number. I'll contact her."

I pulled out my phone and brought up my contact list. April Diaz owned the day care center and I had worked with her on a couple of church committees. I gave the information to Iris, and then said, "Do you know how Ms. Burks is doing?"

"I'm afraid I can't tell you that. That will be up to the doctor."

I was dismissed.

I went over to the waiting area and absently perused the selection of reading materials. Who knew there's a magazine called *Turkey Hunter*? I picked up a three year old issue of *Woman's Day* and chose a chair where I could see the comings and goings to the ER cubicles.

I had been waiting about forty-five minutes when April Diaz walked in. She went directly to Iris' desk and conversed with her for several minutes. When she turned around, she spotted me and came over. April was one of those petite and fragile-looking women who is not to be messed with.

"Lynne, I understand you are the one who found her?"

I explained my acquaintance with Naomi and how I happened to be at her house. "Do you know if she has any family?"

April shook her head. "She only came to town a few months ago. She had a couple of references — individual people — but said she hadn't worked in the last ten years. I did the usual background check and couldn't find any problem but not much other information. I needed help badly so decided to take her on and keep a close eye on her. She's done a wonderful job and the kids love her."

"Really? She doesn't seem like a very warm person."

"She isn't with adults. As far as I know, she has no friends. The other girls and I have invited her to go out for supper with us a couple of times and she always turns us down. But she relaxes more with the kids. Although," April paused and thought a moment, "she's been more upbeat this week than I've ever seen her. Then today, she called in sick for the first time."

"She was planning this, I bet," I said. "She was upbeat because she'd made a decision—to take her own life. How tragic is that?"

April looked stricken. "I had no idea."

"Most people wouldn't. Did she tell you about the friend she lost?"

"No. Nothing personal, ever."

I repeated the story Naomi had told me. "She came to me because her doctor—a shrink, maybe?—told her she needed a vacation. She didn't sound like she really wanted to go. I think she only told me about her friend to explain why she definitely didn't want any kind of wilderness trip."

April sat, shaking her head. "Amazing how little you can know about someone you work with. I've never heard her mention siblings, parents, a husband or children. Not even a pet."

"I didn't see any sign of any of those at her house. No photos or anything."

A doctor came out to Iris' desk, spoke to her, and turned around when Iris pointed at us. He came over.

"Are you Naomi's family?"

April said, "No, I'm her boss. This is the woman who found her. We don't know of any family."

"None at all?" The doctor almost looked like he thought that was our fault. "Well, Iris will continue to pursue that. Meanwhile, since she is obviously a danger to herself, we're going to keep her in the psychiatric wing for a while."

I sat forward. "So she's going to be okay?"

"She's going to survive this, thanks to you. The rest remains to be seen." He nodded and returned to his patients.

April and I hugged each other and as we separated, I wiped tears from my eyes. So did she.

CHAPTER 4

WHEN I REACHED home, I was emotionally wrung out. As I hung up my jacket, Dinah came down from her room.

"Mom! Is she—?"

"She's going to make it but she'll be in the hospital for a while. The big issue right now is to find family or friends. She doesn't seem to have any."

From Dinah's expression, she couldn't imagine such a thing.

"Oh. That's really sad."

"Yes, it is. Is there any more ham left?"

"A little."

"Great. I need a little to make a chef salad. Don't

think I could eat anything heavy. How's the biology coming?"

"Okay. I'm going to work on it a little longer." She turned and went back upstairs.

I felt like I had cut her off abruptly. I wasn't trying to make light of Naomi's predicament—I just needed a little time to recoup and process it all. As I sat on the porch, picking at my salad, I remembered that a couple of weeks before, I had started to do an online search for information on Naomi and never finished. I opened my laptop and typed in her name again.

An entry caught my eye linking to a newspaper notice in Illinois. It was one of those legal notices published in small print. The gist of it was that Naomi Burks was a legal name change for someone formerly known as Melanie Gautier. It was dated March of 2006.

I did a search on Melanie Gautier. There were a number of entries, all ten years old or more. A LinkedIn profile revealed that Melanie had an MBA from the University of Chicago in finance. She held a VP position at a large Chicago bank.

If this was the person I knew as Naomi Burks, how did she go from finance to a day care center? Seemed like a totally different skill set.

Another entry below that was even more intriguing. An article from 2004 reported a police call to a suburban Chicago home where Melanie Gautier had been brutally beaten. Her husband, Tabor, was not home at the time and she could not identify her attacker. A further search revealed no solution to the case.

I sat back in my chair and absently chewed a bite of salad.

"Whatchadoin?" Dinah was back, looking over my shoulder.

"Trying to find out something about my mystery client. To say she has an obscure past is an understatement."

Dinah pulled out a chair and sat down. "What does that mean?"

"First of all," I cautioned her, "none of this is for public consumption." She still looked puzzled, so I added, "not for gossip with your friends, okay?"

"Okay."

"I'm serious. One thing she doesn't need at this point is everyone in town looking at her suspiciously."

"Suspicious of what?"

"Well, that she attempted suicide and that no one knows anything about her."

"So what did you find out?" Dinah nodded toward my laptop. I told her about the name change, the previous job, and the assault.

Dinah's eyes were wide. "And then her friend died? And neither one was ever solved? Mom, you *gotta* go back and find out what's behind all that!"

"No, I don't, for all of the reasons we discussed. And to be accurate, the name change came after the job, the assault, and the loss of her friend."

"Sounds like she was trying to get away from something—or *someone*," Dinah said, lowering her voice in case someone might be listening.

My daughter, the drama queen. "Most likely *something* rather than someone. That's a lot to happen to a person in a couple of years. It's no wonder she's depressed."

"So what happened to her husband?"

"I don't know. I'm guessing they separated or divorced. Some marriages can't hold up to trauma like that." I closed my lap top. "I just wish I knew something that could help her. I'll probably visit her as often as I can —sounds like other than co-workers, no one else is likely to."

Dinah just nodded and looked like she wanted to say more.

THE NEXT DAY, I decided to run over to the hospital on my lunch hour. Being my own boss, sometimes my lunch hour is more than an hour. I didn't have any appointments that afternoon.

My dilemma was whether to inform the hospital of Naomi's previous name. I wanted to talk to Naomi about it first; after all it was really her decision.

Changing one's name is a pretty drastic move. How long does it take before a person quit turning her head at anything that sounds like her old name and begin acknowledging the new one? And all of the accounts, credit cards, and identification that would have to be changed—it boggled my mind. So she must have had compelling reasons to go through all of that.

Iris, on duty again at the intake desk, said that Naomi could not have visitors yet. So my trip was for nothing. Back in my office, I put aside a brochure for a fall leaf trip that I was working on and went back to my computer search.

This time I tried Tabor Gautier. Again, like Melanie, there were a number of references, including the assault story. In June of 2006, an announcement of a wedding between Tabor Gautier and Greta Brown appeared in a Chicago paper. Obviously, Melanie and her husband divorced sometime between the assault and the spring of 2006. A fleeting thought of Greta Gautier made me chuckle—it sounded like a made-up name for a pole dancer.

But a divorce meant there was no point in trying to contact Tabor.

IT WAS FOUR days before I was allowed to see Naomi. She was sitting in an easy chair by the window, staring out at something—or nothing—who knew? When she turned at the sound of my entrance, she didn't register any recognition at first. When she did, it wasn't with any great delight.

"Oh!" she finally said. "Lynne, isn't it?"

"Yes. How are you feeling?" Pretty lame, but I had never to my knowledge visited with someone shortly after a failed suicide attempt. What do you say?

Anger suffused her face. "Did you think I was suddenly going to be okay after you interfered? That my past would be wiped out?"

I was fed up. I knew she had a tragic past but felt I had only done what any one would. "Did *you* think I would just walk out and leave you there?"

"I didn't think you would be in my house! I didn't think *anyone* would walk in without being invited." The scorn in her voice was unmistakable.

This was getting nowhere. "Pardon me," I said. "I assume you are canceling your trip?"

She looked surprised for a moment and then said, "Absolutely. You can keep the deposit."

"Yes, that's the point of a deposit."

"And I'll thank you to stay out of my business."

As I started to turn to leave the room, I couldn't resist one last shot. "Perhaps you can change your name again and start over."

The silence was deafening. She clenched her fists and glared at me. I left before she could respond.

By the time I exited the hospital, I regretted every word. The woman was obviously disturbed and I was overcome with guilt at expecting her to react in a normal way. I turned around and retraced my steps to her room, telling the nurse at the unit desk I had forgotten something. Like my manners and my empathy.

I COULDN'T SEE her at first because she had turned the chair to the window, but I could hear her sobs.

"Naomi?"

Her head snapped up and she peered around the back of the chair. "*Now* what do you want?"

"To apologize. I am very sorry for upsetting you. I *want* to help." It sounded pretty weak, even to me.

"Forget it," she mumbled. "Please just leave me alone."

I sat in a straight back chair at the side of the window where I could look into her face. "It seems to me you need a friend."

She frowned and looked at me like I was dense. "I told you to keep the deposit."

"This isn't about the money or the business. I'm concerned about you. I do care."

"Why?"

"I don't know. Your story when you came to my office was so sad and you were so sad…I don't know what I can do for you, but I'm here. I can imagine how devastating it would be to lose a good friend."

She turned away from me and stared out the window. "Whatever."

"Is it okay if I come back to visit you?"

She shrugged.

"I'll take that as a 'yes'."

No response. So I left the hospital again, feeling slightly less guilty.

CHAPTER

5

OVER THE NEXT week, I stopped at the hospital three times. Each visit, Naomi remained unemotional and deadpan, participating in my feeble attempts at conversation only with monosyllabic answers.

When I returned the following week for a fourth time, I was pleasantly surprised to find Naomi out in the garden courtyard with a weak but very real smile on her face as she read a book to a small child. Judging from the little boy's bare head, I assumed he was a cancer patient. When she looked up, she actually appeared pleased to see me. A little anyway.

I waited patiently until a nurse came for the boy. Naomi promised him another story soon.

"How is he?" I asked, after the nurse and boy were gone.

"Not good. His cancer has come back and the treatments are hard on him." She shook her head. "His nurse keeps telling me how lucky I am to have my health and I know she's right, but I can't help feeling he's the lucky one."

She looked at me for agreement, which I wasn't about to give her. This was the most she had said to me since she had been here.

I sat down on the bench beside her. "What does your doctor say?"

A pause. "The doctor doesn't understand what I've been through."

"Have you told him?"

More silence. "Her. Some of it. I told her about my friend Bev."

"And there's more?"

"A lot more. I don't want to talk about it."

Certainly the death of her friend didn't seem reason for a name change and new identity, but I didn't want to push her. She would just clam up again. "Tell me more about what happened. Was Bev the only camper caught in the flood?"

She shook her head. "There were four women in tents right along the river. They were all caught by the water. One woman managed to grab a branch along the bank. Another was pulled out downstream by a rescue squad."

"So Bev and the other woman weren't found?"

Tears filled her eyes. "I tried to get her to stay with me. I had a little vintage trailer further up the hill and — well, I thought she would be safer, that's all. I should have insisted."

"Why didn't she?" I asked softly.

She ignored my question. "I really appreciate you coming to see me. Especially after I was so rude."

The subject of Bev was closed. I chatted about a couple who were trying to arrange a trip to South America and wrangling over every detail. By embellishing the tale, I even managed to get a couple of smiles out of her.

We got up and walked around the garden, but there were no further references to the cause of her sadness. Instead we focused on a bed of yellow poppies turning their faces to the sun.

A FEW DAYS later, she was released from the hospital to continue treatment as an outpatient. I stopped at her house every other day and got her to go out for supper a couple of times. Occasionally she let slip glimpses of her dark past.

One night we shared a vegetarian pizza at a local joint.

Naomi picked up a piece from the pan, thick cheese stretching between the slices. "Are you married, Lynne? I know you have a daughter but haven't heard you mention a husband."

I was taken aback by her question— only because it was so unusual for her to show interest in anyone outside herself.

"I am, but we have been separated for over a year."

She said, "That's too bad." There wasn't much regret in her voice and she seemed more concerned about getting all of the gooey cheese in her mouth.

"We're going through counseling and making progress. I think we're going to get it worked out."

"Oh." Now she was disappointed. "Well, you're lucky that he's willing to do that. Go through counseling, I mean."

I raised my eyebrows. "Sounds like you're speaking from experience." I picked the green olives off my slice.

She kept her eyes down. "Just what I've seen my friends go through."

"So have you been married?"

"Very briefly. It didn't work out."

But it seemed to require a name change, I thought. That was odd, too—she had never asked me about my name change comment that day in the hospital.

"Any children?" I asked.

"I had one son, Justin."

My heart sank at her words. Another loss?

"I'm so sorry—do you want to tell me what happened?"

She looked at me, startled. "He's alive. I didn't mean that." She sighed. "He played tennis in high school and had a serious shoulder separation. He got hooked on pain relievers and eventually went on to other stuff. His dad did what he could to drive us apart. I think Justin's clean now though."

Just like that. Very matter-of-fact. I thought about the summer before when there was a possibility that I would never see Dinah again because of the time travel. A void threatened to swallow me up just thinking about it. Naomi Burks was very damaged goods.

Another time, I asked her about her college years. She reluctantly admitted she had majored in finance but said the career had too much pressure. I could certainly understand that and perhaps her career change had nothing to do with all the other bad stuff that had happened to her. But perhaps it had.

I BECAME MORE curious about Naomi's marriage. I had quit researching Tabor Gautier when it was evident that there was no reason to contact him about Naomi's hospital stay. Maybe there were more clues to her past there.

Tabor Gautier's LinkedIn page listed his occupation as 'personal trainer.' That surprised me at first. I expected him to be in some kind of power position such as Naomi's. Then I looked at Tabor's description of what he did. His goal, he said, was to release the 'inner alpha' in every man and put each back 'in control of his own life.'

I didn't object to that goal, but there seemed to be

more than a little anti-feminist undercurrent and longing for the good old days of the caveman in the five-paragraph description. He certainly wasn't recruiting any women clients. It sounded like his services would put him in close contact with lots of high-powered types.

"Hey, Mom!" I heard Dinah call from the kitchen and the slam of her books on the kitchen counter.

"Out here on the porch" I felt my chair tilt as she leaned on the back and her curtain of hair fell over my line of sight when she peered over my shoulder at the laptop screen.

"Are you going to get a *personal trainer?*" The disbelief in her voice was understandable. I am not known for dedication to any kind of exercise regimen. I do have good intentions, but unfortunately that doesn't get the heart rate up or the pounds off.

"No, this man is Naomi Burks' former husband."

"The suicide lady?" She dropped into a chair and swiveled back and forth.

"Please don't ever say that in her hearing. As a matter of fact, don't say it at all."

She scoffed. "Of course I wouldn't. Can I see it?"

I slid the laptop in front of her and she scanned the screen. "Sounds like a jerk." She slid the computer back to me.

"Why do you say that?"

"All that alpha male stuff. Don't you think so?"

Huh. She didn't often ask my opinion. "Yeah, I *did* get

that feeling. It's probably just his advertising gimmick."

"Sooo—maybe that's why she changed her name? Maybe he abused her."

I remembered the assault report, and also that Tabor Gautier was out of town at the time.

I said, "That's a leap."

"Without leaps, there would be very few new ideas."

"Who said that?"

"Me." She looked smug. "Think about it. Why would someone change their name? She's hiding from someone. So she's either a serial killer or someone in her past life is looking for her. Do you think she's a serial killer?"

Fifteen-year-old logic exhausted me. "No, I don't. Don't you have homework?"

"Nothing as interesting as this."

"Git!" I said, and received an impish grin as she headed back to the kitchen to get her books.

I DECIDED I needed to talk to Ben Walker. He was the old farmer I had bought the trailer from and he, too, had had time travel experiences with it.

I baked some almond-rhubarb muffins and drove out to Ben's farm. His wife, Minnie waved from her flower garden as I pulled in the drive. She exclaimed over the basket of muffins and ushered me into the house.

"Lynne!" Ben said, and got up from the kitchen table where he had been reading the paper. He gave me a hug. "We've seen you at church but never got a chance to talk to you before you were gone."

"I know. I'm sorry. Life has been crazy the last few weeks."

He poured me a mug of coffee and Minnie pulled out a chair.

"Sit," she said. "You're here now and we're not going to let you go. How's Dinah?"

"Fine—as fine as you can be when you're fifteen." I grinned at them. "I'm sure I was never like that."

"We'll ask your mother." Ben grinned back at me.

"I confess I have an ulterior motive in my visit," I said.

Minnie cocked her head with a puzzled look. "Is there a problem? Nothing serious, I hope."

"Yes and no."

Ben put the basket of muffins on the table, along with plates, knives and a plate of butter.

"Spill," he said. "Yes, there's a problem and no, it's not serious?"

"No, that isn't right either. There's a problem and it's serious. I don't know if I should do anything about it." As I peeled the paper off a muffin and carefully buttered it, I told them about Naomi Burks.

CHAPTER
6

W"OW," BEN SAID, when I had finished. "That's
quite a tale."
"You're thinking of using the trailer to rescue
Naomi's friend," Minnie said.

"That's what I want to talk to you two about. On the
one hand, how can I sit back and do nothing if I can save
this woman's life as well as all of Naomi's grief? On the
other, I'm well aware that trying to change history in the
middle of a flash flood is 'fraught with peril,' as they
used to say on the Saturday matinees."

"That pretty well sums it up," Ben said.

"That's not helping."

"Lynne," Minnie leaned forward over the table and
covered my hand with hers, "First of all, you need to

recognize that the friend's death may not be the root cause of Naomi's depression."

"True. I know it's not that simple. But Naomi has not moved beyond the early stages of grief in ten years. Her boss says she's great with kids, but she certainly doesn't relate well to adults. She seems frightened and sad all of the time."

"You may not realize it yet," Ben said, "but I think you've made your decision."

I sighed. "Maybe. However, I have a lot of questions. When I used the trailer before, I always went back to before I was born. What happens when you go back to a time in your own life? Are there two of you? Minnie, Ben took you back and you stayed. How did that work?"

Minnie gazed at Ben with great love on her face and then back at me.

"We don't know. Some people think the time stream splits. Of course, no one really knows. We reverted to our ages at the time."

"So I would have a problem if I went back to the years before I could drive. But ten years shouldn't be a problem. Do you remember the accident and everything?" I asked.

"Not really. Ben does. Otherwise, he wouldn't have remembered to come back."

I shook my head. "It's too confusing."

"Would you like more coffee?" Minnie asked.

"No, I need to get back." I got up and carried my mug to the sink.

Ben got up too. "I'll walk out with you."

I said my good byes to Minnie and she thanked me again for the muffins. When we got to my car, Ben put a hand on my arm.

"Lynne, think this through very carefully." He swallowed. "I was reckless, not telling you about what the trailer could do when I sold it to you. This sounds like a dangerous situation and something could happen to you."

"I know, and if I do this, I will be very careful. The newspaper accounts that I've found tell which parts of the campground were hit, so I can avoid those. I won't get caught in the flood."

"Well, that's not the only thing that could happen." He gave me a hug. "Actually..." he looked back at the house and took a deep breath. "I didn't take Minnie back. She died from the accident." He shifted back and forth and stuck his hands in his back pockets, looking over his shoulder.

"So you went back and broke up with her? To avoid the accident and save her life?"

"It worked out in our case. Of course I don't know what else I changed in other peoples' lives. Just be careful is all I'm sayin'."

I DECIDED THAT it wouldn't hurt to do some looking for 2005 items I could install in the camper to help me return to the correct year. I had two weeks before the anniversary of the flood. Flooring seemed the most obvious choice but how does one go about finding carpet that is exactly ten years old? And presumably, it would need to be manufactured before June of that year. Maybe a light fixture would be simpler. The more I thought about it, the more confused I got.

I spent the weekend rummaging through a nearby flooring warehouse and haunting thrift shops. One of my problems in this search was how to explain why I wanted something exactly ten years old. Obviously the truth was out of the running.

I thought if I said I was trying to keeps costs down and was looking for things *about* ten years old, I might come across something that would fill the bill. My first bit of luck was at a place offering used housing fixtures to raise money for Habitat for Humanity.

I was not encouraged at first as a young man waited on me, glanced at his phone regularly, and only half-listened to my story. I was therefore surprised when he looked up, snapped his fingers, and then pointed at me.

"You are in luck! Some woman just brought in a truckload of stuff last week. She bought a house that is ten years old and said it was 'dated.'" He nearly dropped his phone trying to do air quotes. "Appliances, carpet, light fixtures — the whole schmozola."

Schmozola? He led me to the back of the store into a warehouse area and my brain was off and running. Appliances? Maybe I could put a microwave in. But I had a niggling sense that it needed to be something more attached to the shell of the camper than that.

My trips the previous summer had occurred when I removed wallpaper, paint and linoleum from the trailer. I wasn't even sure that I could 'manufacture' a time period to travel to.

He pointed to a jumble of goods by the overhead door and then excused himself when the bell over the front door jingled. He left me, looking at his phone the whole time as he headed to the front. I hoped he didn't trip.

I started near the door and looked at kitchen cabinets, bathroom sinks, and railings. I pawed through drapes and blinds. Most of the light fixtures were too large for my needs. In the back were rolls of carpet and pad. I didn't see any vinyl or hard flooring and figured it was probably destroyed in the removal process. Besides, carpet would be easier to remove later.

A lemon yellow short shag had been cut into several smaller pieces. One had the manufacturer's label on the back. Written over the printed logo with a marker was 3/15/05. Could that be a manufacturer's date?

My problem—well, one of my problems—was that I would only get one shot at this before I would have to wait another year. I found one piece that looked like it would fit. My trusty tape measure confirmed my guess. It was slightly dingy so I could say the carpet was there when I purchased the trailer. I didn't want Naomi's friends questioning my taste.

I returned to the store front and negotiated a twenty-five dollar price with the young man. A little steep for the condition but it was for a good cause.

I had made my decision.

I WORKED ON the carpet out at Ben's. I wasn't ready to face Kurt's questions and accusations — mainly because I didn't know the answers myself.

I told myself I could always opt out. Meanwhile, I pored over information about and maps of the Paulie Shoots area. The summer before, I had traveled to a campground and chosen a site away from other campers. I didn't know at first whether my camper disappeared from the present when it time travelled, but I later learned it doesn't.

However, the campground at Paulie's Shoots had been moved to higher ground after the flood, so I decided to travel to a parking lot in the area and spend the night. If I woke up in 2005, I would continue on to Paulie's Shoots and try and get a site.

The walls and ceiling of my 1937 Covered Wagon camper were birch, and Dinah and I had stripped and refinished them. The last thing I had done was expose the original brown and beige tile floor.

The whole inside had a warm glow and I hated the thought of covering that great floor, but it would only be temporary. Last summer, Dinah and I had also picked out several accessories from the Thirties and Forties. Our camper was a very peaceful place. Unless you were wondering what time period you were in.

Ben came out and gave advice on installing the carpet. He offered to help but I knew his health wasn't that great. We decided I should fasten it down using double-sided tape. It was like a blight on the inside surface of that little masterpiece. I hoped Naomi appreciated the sacrifice. Of course, she would never actually know about it.

I WAITED UNTIL the week of my trip to talk to Kurt. It was going to be his weekend to have Dinah, so that worked out well. If Dinah knew I was doing this, she would insist on going.

"I thought you were going to leave this alone," was his first reaction.

"That was before the suicide attempt and her progress — or lack thereof — since."

"I really wish you would reconsider. What if you get caught in this flood?"

This was a huge reversal for Kurt. A couple of years earlier, he would have insisted I not go and stormed out if I didn't agree. He had serious control issues, but we were both making progress.

"I've read all of the news articles about it. I know which part of the campground gets hit. Maybe I can't change anything but I feel I have to try."

He took my hands. "Do you want me to go with you?"

I shook my head. "Sister on the Fly rules say no men. It will be easier for me to be part of the group if I'm alone."

He hugged me. "Please use your head. It won't be good if you save Naomi's friend and Dinah loses her mother."

Now I felt guilty.

CHAPTER 7

I STARTED OUT the day before the Sisters' event at Paulie Shoots. It was gray and dreary, and as I headed south, the west wind tended to push at the trailer. Great. I was nervous enough as it was. I stopped several times for a breather—and coffee—and donuts. This turned out to be a mistake because by noon, a steady drizzle had started and, based on the radar, I was going to be in it for quite a while. I tend to keep a death grip on the steering wheel in less-than-optimum weather and soon began to get cramps in my hands.

The radio doesn't work in my Jeep so I began singing songs from all of the musicals I knew. Alone in the car is the only time I sing, with good reason. My stress increased as I was passed by the behemoth semis so common on the interstates. Sheets of water obscured my vision. I stopped singing in the middle of "I'm Gonna Wash that Man Right Out of My Hair." Sorry, Mr. Rogers and Mr. Hammerstein.

The topography changed from farm fields to rolling hills and back again. As I entered a downhill curve in one of the hilly areas, a large orange truck passed on my left, creating a temporary vacuum that caused the trailer to swing left and then skid back to the right on the rain-slick road. Another semi careening past amplified the motion and I felt the trailer pull the Jeep off toward the side of the road. I gripped the wheel tighter as the Jeep rolled toward the passenger side. I wished I had heeded Kurt's warnings and worries.

When the Jeep finally stopped moving, I was suspended upside-down by my seat belt, which was cutting into my chest and waist. No air bag in this old buggy. I thought I was alive and became aware of someone moving around the front of the Jeep. A young Asian man peered in at me and knocked on the windshield. I feebly raised a hand to let him know I was all right. He held up a phone and pointed to it—I assumed he was calling for help. Then he came around the car and tried with no luck to open my door, which was facing the sky.

For the next several minutes, I crossed my fingers that he actually called 911 and not a gang of thugs to strip me of everything I owned as well as my life. He kept smiling, though, and wore a University of Missouri sweatshirt so I hoped he was just a clean-cut college kid who didn't hang out with thugs.

Approaching sirens calmed my silliness and the next hour was a whirl of police, paramedics, and other emergency personnel. They managed to get me out of the car and onto a stretcher, even though I was sure I could walk. I tried to see about my Jeep and trailer but couldn't turn my head because of the cervical collar. Scott, the young man who had come to my rescue, walked beside the gurney as the EMTs half-wheeled and half-carried it to the waiting ambulance.

"They said it looks like you're going to be fine," he said, and I could hear the worry in his voice. "A wrecker arrived and they will tow your car and trailer to Lurleen —that's the next town and they're taking you there, too. I'm in summer school at Mizzou and going home for a long weekend. I'll be glad to wait around to drive you somewhere or call someone if you want me to."

How sweet. I was ashamed for doubting him.

I said, "No need to do that, my husband will come." And in spite of our problems, I was sure that was true.

"Okay," he said reluctantly. "That looks like a pretty cool trailer."

"It is. Does it look very badly damaged?"

"The part I can see looks okay but of course one side's on the ground. I don't see any parts laying around." He was eagerly trying to find some good news.

I thanked him as the EMTs closed the ambulance

doors and, with a howl, we took off.

EXCEPT FOR BRUISES and one small cut, the doctors and nurses decided I was basically uninjured and told me over and over how lucky I was. I felt every year of my age as I dressed and walked gingerly out of the examining room.

In the clinic lobby, a patrolman waited for me and took down my story for his accident report. Scott was still there and offered me a ride to the garage where my vehicles had been towed. I took him up on it.

I folded myself into his little white Focus. "Thank you for all your help and concern. I might have laid there quite a while. You never know when someone will stop."

"It was nothing." He grinned. "I was getting pretty bored on the drive."

"Well, I appreciate it." I questioned him about his schooling and soon we arrived at a run-down garage named Shorty's near the railroad tracks. A young blonde kid was bent down between my Jeep and the trailer and stood up when he heard our car doors slam.

I was only limping a little. It was still raining so I covered my head with my discharge papers.

"Hi! I'm Lynne McBriar and this is my car and trailer. How bad is it?"

The kid brushed his hair out of his eyes. "The worst part was getting it out of the ditch. Had to get a friend of mine with another wrecker from Burnsville. That trailer is something—pretty well built. Only big problem was your hitch—all twisted to beat hell. That's not a common size. But my boss had one in his garage and we put it on for ya. Got the other in the office if you want to see it."

"No, I believe you. I thought it would be much worse. How much do I owe you?"

"The bill's in the office."

My guardian angel Scott said goodbye and got back on the road. I followed the mechanic to the office and he showed me the twisted hitch anyway. After paying the bill, I took my keys to the trailer, dreading what I would find inside.

Again, I was pleasantly surprised. The refrigerator-style latches had kept all of the cabinets closed except one, and it only held extra bedding. The cushions were on the floor and there were a few messes in the icebox but considering the accident, I felt fortunate. I straightened the other cabinets, cleaned the icebox as best I could and locked the trailer again.

Back in my Jeep, I leaned my head back and took a deep breath. My bruises were starting to clamor for attention.

What was I doing? Should I call Kurt? Should I head back home?

The rain was persistent, and I wasn't anxious to get back on the road. But I had a feeling that my accident was not as bad as it could have been for a reason. If I called Kurt, he would try and talk me back home or come and join me. Yet the thought of getting back on the road in the rain turned my stomach.

I pulled out my map—the paper kind—and found Lurleen. I needed a campground that had been in existence without changes for at least ten years. Preferably one with some isolated sites.

I found a state park a few miles down the road that looked like just the ticket. I pulled up the park website on my iPad and looked at the campground map. The campground photos showed sites tucked in among thick woods. I would check it out.

CHAPTER 8

A

T THE ENTRANCE, I pulled over and walked up to the check-in station. A nice woman in a DNR shirt acted like I was her long-lost friend.

She pulled a campground map from a stack and then scrutinized my face. "Honey — what happened to *you*?"

I touched a bruise on my cheek. "I had a little accident back a ways — put the Jeep and the trailer in a ditch on their sides." I gave her a 'what-can-you-do?' shrug. "I planned to go farther today but I think I need a good night's sleep."

"In the ditch? Are you sure, honey? I work with the women's shelter and — "

I saw where she was going with this and briefly envisioned the cops picking a bewildered Kurt up and hauling him off to the pokey. I put a palm up to stop her. "No, really. Look at the side of my trailer. See all of the twigs and grass stuck to it? I got caught in the backwash of a semi on a curve in the rain. The clinic in Lurleen looked me over and a good mechanic replaced my hitch. No other damage."

"Oh, good. I mean, not that you had an accident, but I see so many abused women, honey. Was that Shorty's Garage? They're so good there."

"They did a great job," I agreed.

"Well, let's find you a great site." She pulled a campground map out of the stack and consulted a master taped to the counter.

"How long has this campground been here?"

She scratched her forehead with the end of her pen. "Well, honey, a long time. The sites are pretty old and they keep telling us they're going to redo the campground but we aren't busy enough to be very high on the list."

Perfect, I thought. Thank goodness for slow legislatures.

She circled several sites with a red pen. "These are the sites that are occupied. We're only about half full since it's the middle of the week. This one's nice and close to the bathrooms and this one has a view of the lake."

"What about that one?" I pointed to the end of the road.

"That one's kind of isolated." She went on to mark other sites.

"That will be fine. I really need the quiet."

She raised her eyebrows and sighed, frustrated that I wasn't willing to let her mother me. She handed me the registration form and I filled it out.

She wasn't giving up. She circled the office phone number with her red marker on the campground rules and said "You be sure and call if you need anything. I'll be on 'til 9:00 tonight. And my camper is in site #1."

"Thank you for your concern. I'll be fine. I hope to be asleep long before 9:00. I need the spot through the weekend."

I knew from experience that the trailer didn't disappear from the present. But I had never tried to move once I had gotten to another time period. So just in case, I thought I should save the spot and try and return to the present in the same spot.

My head started to hurt as I realized the weakness of my logic — holes big enough to drive a trailer through. Okay Scarlett — think about that tomorrow.

THE SITE SAT at an angle at the end of the road. A row of small trees and shrubs lined each side, concealing it until I reached the turn. I did not unhitch the trailer since I didn't plan to go anywhere and went inside, tempted to throw myself on the couch and collapse. I was afraid I would fall asleep and had several tasks I needed to do before that reward.

I checked the time — Kurt would not be home from

work yet, so I began straightening the cupboards. There were some casualties among the spices—as if I was going to actually cook something— but the clothes, canned goods, and pots and pans just needed rearranging. Then I sat down and pulled out my phone. Kurt picked up on the first ring.

"Hey! Wondered if I was going to hear something."

"I actually stopped sooner than I expected. It was really tiring driving in the rain." I didn't mention the accident, but told him about the park I was in.

"It was there ten years ago and the same configuration?"

"I think so. I asked if it was old and she said yes and that plans to redo the campground had been put on hold indefinitely. I couldn't really come out and ask her if the site I chose was in the same spot ten years ago."

"I guess not," he said. "What if someone is camped there 10 years ago?"

"I don't know. There's no way I can know, but it's the most isolated site. I think that the big storm that flooded Paulie's Shoots affected this area too, and that would have discouraged campers."

He was quiet a moment. "How will you explain being there when you check out tomorrow morning?"

"Most campgrounds don't require you to check out. I can just leave." I changed the subject. "How's Dinah?"

"Haven't seen her since I got home. She was scheduled to work tonight at the pool."

I slapped myself in the forehead. "Forgot that. Well, tell her I called and love you both."

"Really?" he laughed. "Don't you expect to make it back?"

The frustrations of the day rushed over me and tears filled my eyes. Was that what I thought deep down?

"I'll be back. I'm not gonna let you guys off that easily," I said with more confidence than I felt.

After I hung up, I sat and let self-pity and self-reproach invade my bones. Why didn't I say goodbye to Dinah?

I had so many questions about how this would work. I wasn't even sure that I could place myself in 2005. I had a charm bracelet with a commemorative Christmas charm on it with that year—I was assuming that it had been made earlier the same year but had no way of actually knowing. The jewelry thing was just a theory anyway. For that matter, so was the remodeling.

At this point, on every trip with this trailer, I considered the choice before me. I could tow the trailer back into Lurleen, find a cheap little motel, and head back home in the morning. I could go back to my family and friends and avoid this trip fraught with uncertainties.

My accident was a perfect and legitimate excuse to abandon this venture. Then Naomi's grief-stricken face filled my thoughts.

I had to go through with this.

THE NEXT MORNING, I lay there once again wondering about the year. On previous trips, the time change was obvious when I looked outside because enough years had rolled by to make the landscape different. That might not be the case this morning.

So I looked outside and thought the trees might be smaller but couldn't be sure. After dressing and a little breakfast, I readied the trailer for travel and went outside. One definite difference was that the sun was out. That was a relief; I didn't relish driving another day in the rain. I took a chance and wired some old 2005 license plates over mine. I had found them in one of the junk stores at home.

As I pulled out of the campsite, I chided myself for not paying closer attention to the other campers that had been in the campground the night before. I passed the registration shack and waved to the older man in the window. I resisted the temptation to ask him what year it was. People look at you funny if you do that.

A few miles down the road, I came to a convenience store. Good spot to fill up my coffee mug and buy a paper. I steeled up my courage to look at the date and was both relieved and anxious to find that it was 2005.

It occurred to me as I returned to my Jeep, that I hadn't even looked in the mirror that morning. The little bathroom mirror in the trailer was cloudy and discolored so I seldom used it. When I brushed my teeth, I was so absorbed in the question of the date, that I didn't think to check and see if I looked ten years younger. Now that I thought of it, my shorts did feel a little looser. Ben had said that he reverted to his former self.

By the time I turned off the interstate onto a two-lane state highway, the sunshine and rolling hills lifted my mood considerably. The road wound through the hills. Traffic was light and I took my time, enjoying the scenery. As I drove through a tunnel formed by overhanging trees in infinite shades of green and dappled by the sun, it was hard to imagine that the upcoming weekend held disaster at the hands of Mother Nature.

CHAPTER
9

THE ENTRANCE TO Paulie's Shoots led down a winding narrow road into a valley ringed by stone bluffs and steep hills. Signs pointed to a campground that rambled along the edge of the fast moving White Fox River. It was easy to see, with my hindsight, how a flash flood could wreak devastation.

I stopped at the host site and knocked on the screen door of a fairly new fifth wheel. The campsite, like many host sites, boasted a wide variety of yard ornaments, from pinwheels to a carved wooden sign that said 'Welcome to the Hautmanns—Cal and Lil.' A short woman, probably ten years older than me, came to the door wiping her hands on a dish towel.

"Hi!" she said. "Can I help you?"

"I'm looking for a camping spot for the next three days. Have you got anything?"

"Oh, I'm not sure." She opened the door. "Come in. Cal!" She called, toward the back of the camper. "Are there any walk up sites left for this weekend?"

Cal came down the steps from the bedroom area. "A couple of small ones. What kind of rig?" he asked me.

"A small trailer," I said and grinned. "It's a 1937 Covered Wagon."

His eyebrows shot up. "No kidding?"

"Are you with the Sisters on the Fly?" Mrs. Cal said.

"No, I heard some were going to be here. They have some great vintage trailers, don't they?"

"They sure do. This is the third year they've been here for this weekend."

"I'll get my shoes and show you what we've got. Good thing you're here today; those sites will be gone by tomorrow," Cal said.

Soon we were back outside. After stopping to admire my trailer, he hefted himself into a golf cart and told me to 'hop in.'

"No point in dragging your rig around because these two sites are at opposite ends of the campground."

I joined him with my interpretation of a hop—which did *not* involve both feet leaving the ground at the same time—and we lurched off toward the lower end of the campground.

"The Sisters on the Fly will be mostly down here," he

said. We pulled up at site #48. It was small, although big enough for me, but near the river in quite a low area. Knowing what I did, I had no desire to be that close to the river. I did see several vintage trailers and a couple of tents already set up in nearby sites.

"Well, I'm not a member and don't want to seem like I'm intruding. Where is the other one?"

He shrugged and said, "Back up the hill. Not much of a view of the river."

"That's okay. Do you mind?"

"'Course not." And off we went.

Site #122 was three rows up and also looked like it would be easier to back into. I used that as an additional reason for my choice. "I don't have a lot of experience yet."

Cal smiled. "Good decision, then. I like a woman who knows her own limits."

Somehow it didn't come off as a compliment, but no matter. Soon I had filled out the registration and was back in my Jeep pulling my trailer to #122.

I was glad that Cal was occupied elsewhere and missed my parking demonstration. There was no physical damage, but it was not a thing of beauty. After several back-and-forths, jumping out to check my progress, and more back-and-forths, I called it good and proceeded with my setup.

On previous trips, I had to think about clothes, technology, book covers—all sorts of issues that would raise questions. This time, shorts, jeans and tee shirts were as ubiquitous in 2005 as 2015. I had carefully avoided any tee shirts sporting 2008 campaign slogans. And I wasn't as nervous about making some faux pas that would mark me as out of place (and time.)

After my setup, I decided to check out the whole campground. I knew that Naomi and her friend Beverly would be arriving later that day.

As I walked by one of the vintage trailers, a woman was hanging a string of flags made of red and yellow flowered prints along her awning. Under the awning, two red metal lawn chairs with yellow gingham cushions sat on a black and white checked outdoor rug. A sign stuck in the ground proclaimed "Sisters on the Fly — We Have More Fun Than Anyone."

While I watched, she finished, got down from a little step-stool, and stepped back to judge the results.

"Looks great," I said.

She turned around. "Oh, hi. Thank you. Are you a Sister?"

I was pretty sure she didn't mean 'nun.' "No but I've read about your group. It *does* sound like you have more fun than anyone."

She grinned and held out her hand. "I'm Glynis Wiggins."

"Lynne McBriar. Do you have a big group coming for the weekend?"

"About twenty. There's usually some last minute

changes." She looked up at the sky. "I hope the weather holds. There's some prediction of heavy rains Saturday. We've got some kayaking and fishing events planned."

I could have enlightened her on that, but didn't want her to call in the little men in white coats.

"Sounds like fun."

She brushed off her hands. "I'm ready for a break. Could I interest you in a glass of tea?"

"That would be wonderful."

Sitting in the old metal chairs under the cheery awning and watching the river rush past, I could almost forget the tragedy that was due to play out before the weekend was over. "This is lovely. How did you get involved with this group?"

"My cousin joined down in Texas and got me interested. My husband was killed in Iraq—lifetime military, so I'm pretty used to trying things on my own. I found this old Shasta in a local junkyard and my daughter helped me fix it up. She's an electrician," she finished proudly.

"Handy skill to have," I said.

"Absolutely. I named her Louella—the trailer, not my daughter. Rhymes with *Red and Yella, Kiss a Fella*. Want to see inside?"

"I'd love to." I'd been admiring a group of red plaid thermoses in assorted sizes arranged on the lid of an old picnic basket. "Doesn't it take a long time to set all of this stuff up?"

She looked around and smiled. "Longer than some would want to bother with, but only about half an hour. It just makes me feel good to be surrounded by cheerful stuff, so it's worth it." She led the way up a couple of steps.

Inside, one end was taken up with a dinette table and benches. The furniture and walls were all painted white. The cushions were covered in red vinyl and the table topped with yellow laminate. Throw pillows and curtains in red window pane check and yellow florals continued the theme. The rest of the interior included a sofa bed on one side and a kitchenette on the other. Artfully placed accessories—kitchen utensils and other useful items—caught the eye everywhere one looked. There was a friendly order to the clutter.

"It's just great. How long did it take you to do this?"

"A little over a year."

"It's amazing. You did a wonderful job."

A voice called from outside. "Yoohoo, Glynis! Time to party, girl!"

Glynis cringed a little. "I know that voice. It's Gloria Reveley and she gets a little carried away sometimes."

I peeked over her shoulder as she opened the door ahead of me. A woman in a large cowboy hat festooned with feathers and rhinestones was standing in the road holding a martini glass. She wore a western shirt, also black, and a full hot pink crinoline over blue jeans and boots.

I checked my watch—it wasn't even noon yet.

"Glorie," Glynis said. "Starting a little early?"

Gloria raised her glass. "It's never too early." It seemed like it might already be too late, the way she was slurring her words.

Glynis introduced me. Gloria inquired whether I was a Sister and was I interested in joining and what kind of camper did I have or was I tent camping and so on. One of those people who asked a question and then interrupted your answer to ask another question. I finally excused myself to continue my walk.

"Stop back later when more are here," Glynis said, her eyes full of apology. "We'll have a cocktail hour about 5:00 and there's some great women in this group."

I couldn't tell if she was including Gloria in that group.

I WAS ANXIOUS to scope out the site that Naomi would be staying in. She, of course, would not know me. Green cards with the names of the reservation holders were on the site posts, so I hoped to see where she was going to be located before she arrived. Less obvious, I thought, than peering at the posts later of every occupied site.

I finally located a post with the name 'Gautier' written in marker on the card. Naomi wouldn't be changing her name for another year—something I needed to remember. The site was on the road below mine and closer to the entrance. I continued down to the tent sites closer to the river and also found a card labeled 'Borcherd.'

That settled, I returned to my camper to fix some lunch. It was always a relief that time travel didn't seem to affect the food in my vintage ice box. With a turkey sandwich on whole grain bread and piled with fresh lettuce and tomatoes, I was feeling pretty smug, as though good health was already coursing through my veins.

My picnic table was under the shade of a large old linden and I had covered it with a 1930's tablecloth from the local junk store. Sitting there and looking down on the rest of the campground, I regained some of the contentment and security I had felt sitting in front of Glynis' trailer. Nostalgia satisfies.

I had checked before I left and since Kindles wouldn't be marketed for two years yet, I left mine at home and brought an old hard copy of *Giants in the Earth*, one of my favorites. It was very pleasant sitting, reading, and watching the campground gradually fill up as the afternoon progressed.

I kept an eye toward Naomi's site and about half-way through the afternoon, saw a turquoise and white Franklin being backed in — much more smoothly than my own sad attempt.

I couldn't see the woman driving clearly but her general appearance certainly jived with what I knew of

Naomi. Her movements, however, showed much more energy and purpose than I had ever seen Naomi exhibit.

Another woman was with her — I assumed the unfortunate Beverly. After the trailer was unhitched and set up completed, they both got back in the small pickup and continued down by the river. There my view was partly obscured by other units but I could see enough to tell a tent was being set up.

I looked at my watch. Four o'clock. I believed I would join the cocktail hour. I put my book away and went inside to mix up some spinach dip to share.

CHAPTER 10

I SLIPPED INTO clean shorts, sandals, and a lime green tee shirt. With standard campground etiquette, I took along a lawn chair and a can of beer, plus my dip and a bag of chips. About a dozen women had gathered in front of Glynis' trailer and most appeared to know each other. The scraps of conversation floating around on the warm late afternoon breeze were of the 'How've you been?' variety sprinkled with questions about kids, dogs, and even husbands.

Some were decked out in western gear and some in shorts or jeans and neon green tee shirts that said "Shoot the Shoots-2005" with wavy lines representing water below it. There were outrageous hats and necklaces with feathers and camouflage pants with lace ruffles sewn around the bottom.

My first close encounter was with a petite woman with short red hair. She was drinking something pink out of a canning jar and she grabbed my chair and unfolded it.

"Put your snacks over there." She motioned to a card table covered with, of course, a red and yellow flowered tablecloth. She held out her hand. "I'm Teri Crowley."

I introduced myself. Glynis spotted me from the other side of the group and waved.

"Are you a new Sister?" Teri asked. "I don't think we've met before."

"No, I'm staying in the campground and Glynis invited me to join the cocktail hour."

"Well, you can be a SOTT for the weekend."

I laughed. "A sot? That doesn't sound good."

"A Sister on the Try. You're allowed to take part in an event once without joining. See if you like it. Besides, Glorie is our resident drunk." She nodded toward a chair by the trailer. I could see the woman I met earlier and she wasn't going to last the whole hour. "Where are you from?" Teri asked.

"Southeast Iowa." I looked around at the rest of the group. "Are all of these women from Missouri or other states too?"

"Missouri, Iowa, Illinois, Arkansas—one or two from Nebraska, I think."

I spotted Naomi in the middle of the group. Even allowing for dropping ten years, I could hardly believe it was the same person. She was laughing out loud and there was a sparkle in her eyes. I couldn't say that she was completely relaxed but at least much happier than I had ever seen her.

I didn't really have a plan. I could just stand back and try to be in a position to observe until action was necessary. Or I could contrive to meet her and Bev; it would probably be easier to stay close without raising questions.

So for the next twenty minutes, Teri introduced me around and eventually we got to Naomi/Melanie. She of course showed no recognition but greeted me warmly.

Beverly Borcherd was next to her, a tall, gangly woman—pretty although not a ravishing beauty. She wore khaki cargo shorts, a "Shoot the Shoots" shirt, and a Cubs baseball cap. Shoulder length brown hair was pulled back behind her ears under the cap.

We chatted about where we were from and what kind of camping equipment we had. I told them about my Covered Wagon and received stares of awe.

"I want a tour," Bev said. "I have my eye on a couple of old trailers but can't decide. I'm still making do with my tent."

She wouldn't be making do with the tent in a couple of days though.

Melanie grinned and said, "I've been trying to find

her a trailer for a couple of years but she is soooo picky."

"Right. Because I don't want a rat's nest in it or a floor like a sponge?"

"That's the *fun* part, Bev—fixing it up. I had to replace the whole floor in mine, you know."

"Ha!" Bev said. "You replaced it with my help. You'll probably disappear when it's time for my project."

"Now, girls—do I have to separate you?" Teri laughed, and it was obvious that they were all used to this long-standing argument.

Melanie's face changed as a late model maroon BMW cruised slowly along the road. She paled and ducked behind me. Bev took a quick glance back at the road and jerked back.

"What's he doing here?" she muttered to Melanie.

"Checking on me, I suppose," was the muffled reply.

"Is something wrong?" I asked.

Melanie shook her head. "My husband is a little controlling," she said. Her laugh and shrug said it was no big deal. And probably none of my business. But her cheerful facade had been dampened and she moved quickly toward the little red and yellow trailer. "I'll go see if Glynis needs any help."

Teri said, "Are you joining us for supper, Lynne?"

"Oh I don't think so."

"Sure you are." Bev hooked her arm in mine and started leading me over to Gynis. "We're having a potluck and there is always *way* too much food. You can bring your own table service or I've got extra."

"I have some brownies," I said. "Can I contribute those?"

Bev turned serious. "We don't usually do dessert. You know so many are dieting and some have allergies…"

"She is one humungous liar," Teri said. "We live for dessert and would love your brownies."

Glynis came out of her camper carrying a large red bowl covered with foil. Bev told her that I was joining them for supper and would be bringing brownies.

"Great!" Glynis said. "I was going to suggest it. I mean, joining us for supper, not bringing brownies. Not that I don't *love* brownies. You know what I mean."

IT WAS AN interesting and pleasant evening. The slight breeze kept the bugs off and the temperature bearable. Supper included great pasta salads, homemade rolls, fruit, and fried chicken.

The variety of backgrounds of the Sisters intrigued me. Melanie still had her banking job, Glynis was a vet's assistant, Teri a housewife, and Victoria Lenihan sitting across from me worked for a car dealership. Bev had the consulting firm and also worked in a convenience store at night—I assumed that meant the consulting wasn't going so well.

Several women had or were facing major crises in their lives. Teri had a 35-year-old disabled son living at home. Victoria was a breast cancer survivor. Glynis was widowed and cared for two young grandchildren while her daughter—a single mom—worked.

I knew Melanie had issues but she didn't talk about them. Several had been through job changes recently. Through it all, they were wonderfully supportive of each other.

Glorie fell asleep in her lawn chair and two women helped her to her camper and put her to bed. Glynis said, "Obviously, she has a huge problem. We have talked about doing an intervention but her family is against it."

"Why?"

Glynis shrugged. "She's seeing a shrink who says her depression has to be dealt with before addressing the alcoholism."

"Alcohol *is* a depressant."

"I know. It's very hard. We only have her word for it that the doctor told her that. Her family means well so it's difficult to interfere. We may decide to anyway."

Much of the talk centered on plans for kayaking the next day.

"Have you been here before?" Victoria asked.

"No, my first trip. How did the place get its name?"

"You mean, Shoots? Paulie was the name of the man who owned the land and when the state took it over years ago, apparently someone in the office thought chutes was spelled 's-h-o-o-t-s.' It's stayed that way ever since. The chutes are narrow passages down river that are like water slides. We don't kayak through those."

"They aren't far from the campground, are they?"

Victoria shook her head. "No, it's a short walk. I could show you after supper."

"That would be great."

We finished eating and everyone busied themselves clearing their food and dishes. I took mine back up the hill to my trailer after making plans to meet Victoria by the river in fifteen minutes. Long enough to brush my teeth and change into walking shoes.

THE PATH LED right along the edge of the rushing river. A short distance from the campground, granite cliffs began appearing along the banks and boardwalks consisting of steps and platforms were built into the cliff along our side of the river.

What had been a distant rumble increased to a low roar as we neared the 'Shoots.' The river narrowed and twisted and was strewn with huge gray granite boulders — some jagged and others worn smooth by the water. Small shrubs and trees struggled to maintain purchase in the crevices of the cliffs. We climbed the steps of one of the boardwalks and leaned on the railing of one of the highest platforms watching the setting sun sparkle off the water.

"Beautiful," I said.

Victoria pointed at a couple of pools formed by the rocks that looked almost like natural tubs. "Lots of people like to sit in those pools on really hot days. And see how those rocks form natural water slides?"

I nodded. The water pounded through the rocks in a comforting rhythm. We watched several butterflies check out an elderberry bush growing out of the bank right below the platform. The peace of the place was a huge counter balance to the stress I'd been feeling lately. Maybe everything would work out and I could do some good here.

A crash behind me shook us and the platform we stood on, echoed off the bluffs, and shattered my contentment.

"What?" Victoria yelled and whirled around. I had grabbed the railing, feeling like something was going to throw me over onto the rocks below.

"Oh my God!"

I turned around. A large boulder lay on the platform not two feet behind me.

CHAPTER

11

We both looked up at the cliff above us. I hadn't seen any signs for falling rocks.

"Oh my God!" Victoria said again. "Are you okay?"

"Yeah, other than a little weak in the knees. And a pounding heart."

"I've never heard of any falling rocks here." She stared at the culprit. "We'd better report it to the ranger."

She led the way back along the boardwalk and path, and I could hardly keep up. My heart continued to pound and my hands were shaking so bad, I kept my fists clenched. We both stumbled a little bit as we hurried.

"How do we find a ranger?" I said.

"We'll have the host contact the ranger office."

We slowed down as we got to the campground. Some of the shock was wearing off.

Victoria put her hand on my arm as we walked. "That was so close."

As if I had forgotten. "They probably need to close the boardwalk."

As we neared the host's campsite, I noticed a late model maroon BMW pulling away. Tabor Gautier? Couldn't be too many of that kind of car tooling around any given campground. Interesting.

Mrs. Cal—Lil—was standing outside, apparently having just visited with the driver of the BMW.

Victoria wasted no time. "Ms. Hautmann, we had a scare on the boardwalk." She described the event. "We couldn't see anywhere above us that it might have come from. Have there been rock falls in that area before?"

Lil Hautmann shook her head. "Never that I know of."

"Could you let the ranger's office know?" I asked. "Maybe they need to close the boardwalk until they figure out the problem."

"You're right. I'll let them know right away." She pulled her cell out of her pocket. We waited until she finished.

She closed her phone. "Thanks for letting us know. By the way, isn't Melanie Gautier part of your group?"

"Yes. Why?"

"You might tell her that her husband was looking for her. Apparently he hasn't been able to get her on the phone."

I looked at Victoria to see her reaction. I could detect a little concern on her face. "Is it an emergency?"

"Well, he didn't say whether it was or not."

"We'll tell her. Thanks."

We walked back toward Glynis' site.

"What's the deal with Melanie's husband?" I asked. "I saw that same car go by during the cocktail hour and I know Melanie saw it too."

Victoria sighed. "It's very complicated and I don't know the whole story. I do know that he objects to Mel's friendship with Beverly."

"Why?"

"Well, she was the one involved in that whistle-blowing incident." Seeing my confusion, she added, "You know, that Bailoff drug company? She was a chemist for them and went to the feds about some trials that had been tweaked?"

I had read the story but didn't want to appear too well-informed. "Why did Melanie's husband care about that?"

"Some of the Bailoff bigwigs are his clients."

We were nearing Glynis' campfire and about a dozen women sat around, including Melanie and Beverly. Laughter drifted up with the smoke. The firelight picked out the faces in the waning evening light.

Glynis called out. "How was your walk?"

"More eventful than we had in mind," Victoria recounted our unwanted adventure.

"Oh, my gosh!" a tall woman with long dark hair said. I think her name was Julie something. "I've never heard of a problem with falling rocks here."

"Although, I guess those boulders must have gotten in the river somehow," said another.

"Actually, most of them were formed by water erosion, not falling from the cliff," Teri said.

"Sounds like you were very lucky," Glynis said. "Better sit down and have a drink."

Victoria pulled a lawn chair over by Melanie. Once seated, she leaned over and quietly told Melanie about her husband. She nodded without much expression. The conversation picked up again and Melanie seemed to be unconcerned about the wishes or whereabouts of her mate.

The woman named Julie was in the middle of a convoluted, hilarious story about a raccoon in her tent on an earlier trip, when a ranger's truck pulled up. A middle-aged man in a ranger uniform got out and walked toward the group.

"Good evening," he said. "Who are the women who saw the rock fall?"

Victoria and I raised our hands.

"We didn't actually see it," Victoria said. "We were standing by the railing watching the river when it landed behind us. It barely missed Lynne."

"Did you hear anything—any other rocks falling at the same time?"

We both shook our heads. "We didn't hear anything until it crashed behind me," I said.

He looked in the direction of the Shoots as if he had x-ray vision. "We checked up at top of that bluff but can't tell where it came from. That doesn't prove anything, of course; just that we can't see a problem area. There are some tracks up there so we're investigating the possibility that someone caused it, probably accidentally. We're going to close the boardwalk until we can get some signs up. It's always a risk in this type of terrain."

"I understand," I said.

After he left, the group buzzed with speculation.

Bev finally spoke up. "I think we all need to be extra careful this weekend." She paused and looked at the group. "I haven't told anyone else this, but I've received several threats lately. Because of the whistle-blowing, you know. They're boycotting my business."

Questions flew at her from all sides.

"Have you told the police?"

"Bev, why didn't you say something?"

"You need to report it!"

"What kind of threats?"

Glynis objected. "But Bev, you weren't there. Why would you think someone was targeting you?"

"Lynne and I are dressed similarly. From above, it would be hard to tell us apart."

She was right. We both had lime green shirts and khaki shorts and our hair was a similar color and style. I shivered, considering the possibility that my big scare was intentional.

"How would they even know where you were?" Victoria asked.

Bev looked at Melanie. "Tabor might tell them," Melanie said. "He was driving around here earlier."

I decided to jump in. "I don't understand. What happened with the whistle-blowing?"

Bev sighed and fiddled with her pony tail. "Short story: I worked for a pharmaceutical company and they fudged some trials on a new drug. I told the FDA and lost my job."

"I thought they couldn't do that."

"Legally, they can't, but if someone wants you out, there are ways. I haven't been able to get a job anywhere else in my field. So I started my own consulting firm. And like I said, no one is darkening my door."

"Bev, make sure this weekend that you aren't alone. Always be with a group," Victoria said.

"Thanks for your concern but being with someone didn't help you and Lynne much, did it?"

The group was silent for a few moments. Finally, Glynis said, "Well, tomorrow, we're kayaking, right? Who all is going?"

I said, "I've never been in a kayak. I've canoed—is it similar? That is, if I'm allowed to join you?"

"Absolutely," Glynis said. "You can be a Sister on the Try for the whole weekend. Take part in any of our activities you want. And if you've canoed, you'll have no problem."

"Thank you." In the back of my mind, I recalled several unfortunate incidents in my life when someone had told me 'no problem.'

Although some of the Sisters had brought their own kayaks, Glynis filled me in on the cost and plans for kayak rentals and offered to call the rental place in the morning to add one for me. I agreed.

SHORTLY, I DECIDED my near miss with the rock had stressed me more than I realized and I longed for my bed. I said my good nights and headed up the hill. There was a lot to think about.

I met two couples taking a late night walk, gazing at the moon and stars and sharing private jokes. My first thought was that I missed Kurt. He has never been interested in camping, or much outdoor activity for that matter. His only experience with this trailer the summer before didn't give him much of a taste of camping since the trailer had time-travelled inside a barn.

I exchanged greetings with the two couples and was passing them, when one of the men stopped me.

"Say! Are you with that group of gals down there?" He nodded in the direction of Glynis' campfire.

Rather than explain the subtle differences of being a Sister on the Try, I said, "Yes."

"What do they do? They don't have any husbands?"

I wasn't sure where he was coming from. "Some do, but one of their rules is 'No men' at most of their events."

"What are they, a bunch of — ?"

"Gary," his wife cautioned. "Be nice."

"It's just a group of women who enjoy out-of-door activities," I said. "They have several of these events a year."

The wife smiled at me as she took her husband's arm to lead him away. "Sorry. He's had a few too many beers. Nice evening."

Maybe I didn't miss Kurt.

CHAPTER 12

I WENT TO BED still wearing the bracelet with the 2005 charm to, I hoped, assure I stayed in 2005. Still, it was a relief the next morning to look out and see the same campers around me. The sun was climbing in a clear blue sky. It would be a great day to be on the river.

Glynis had warned me to "dress to get wet" — a little unnerving after seeing the rocks in the river. I donned an old swimsuit and added baggy shorts and a loose t-shirt.

The night before, Julie had invited all comers to breakfast. Since I had stuffed myself at supper, I opted for some fruit, granola, and yogurt. That would allow me to feel smug when I indulged in the treats several were bringing on the river trip.

As I ate at the picnic table and watched the early stirrings in the campground, I mulled over Melanie and Bev's situations. It occurred to me that it was odd that Tabor Gautier would have come all of the way from Chicago to southern Missouri to check on his wife. They wouldn't be divorced for another year, but perhaps this kind of control would be a contributing factor.

When I got down to Glynis' camper, a pickup had arrived pulling a trailer with seven or eight brightly colored kayaks. The group planned to put in below the 'Shoots' and the rental outfit would come back in the afternoon to the take-out point to pick up their equipment.

Glynis was talking to a young man by her trailer and signing something on a clipboard. His shaggy, straight brown hair barely covered his ears but almost concealed his eyes. A navy t-shirt with 'Coyotes' in faded white letters stretched across his well-built back.

Glynis handed him the clipboard and he stuck the pen in a back pocket of his tight jeans. He nodded good-bye and jogged back to the pickup, followed by several pair of wistful eyes. The truck pulled away, dragging the rack of rattling kayaks.

Glynis smiled and shrugged as I approached her. "He was a little confused about where he was supposed to meet us. I hope he doesn't have the same trouble with the take-out point. It's a good thing he's so cute."

"You really think I can do this?" I noticed the helmet she held by the straps and the life vest she wore.

She laughed. "Don't worry. We'll give you some instruction when we start. That's why I told you to wear something that could get wet."

Now I *was* worried, but Glynis turned to greet some of the other Sisters and arrange car pools to the put-in point. I climbed in a pickup with Teri and Victoria. We bumped along back roads to an almost hidden dirt track between two pastures. A few cows and a horse eyed us suspiciously as we bounced toward the river.

The put-in had a slightly shallower bank and a wide area where women were already removing kayaks from vehicles or helping the young man to unload the trailer. Lazy dragonflies flitted along the river's edge, which itself appeared pretty slow-moving in this spot. My hopes raised at the sight. Then I thought of Kurt arguing that something other than the coming flood could endanger me — like a kayak float maybe?

Glynis referred to a list of the women who had reserved a rented kayak and determined that there was one extra. The young man put it back on the trailer and left the area.

Glynis blew sharply on a silver whistle that she wore around her neck. The chattering quieted and everyone looked at her.

"Before we start, we have three novices who need a little instruction. Lynne, Mercy, and Debra — we're going to show you how to do a wet exit and how to paddle. If you've canoed, the paddling won't be difficult but the wet exit is a different story." The non-novices cheered at the mention of a wet exit and my hopes sank again.

What followed was, as they say, not pretty. They swore it wasn't hazing but they got us into kayaks, sealed the spray skirts, and gave us enough paddling instruction to get us to a deep hole along the bank. One by one, we were instructed how to roll the kayak and try to right it. If not successful (and none of us were), we learned how to pop the spray skirt and extract ourselves from the boat to get back to the surface.

We were told never to try and stand up in the river to avoid getting a foot caught, to hang on to our paddles if possible, and how to tow the boat back to shore. All of this was accompanied by cheers, encouragement, and a few laughs from those still along the bank.

We returned to the put-in spot soaking wet and filled with the glory of accomplishment. The launch was mass confusion with kayaks knocking together and scraping along the rocks, laughter, and shouts of caution. Once the flotilla started down the river, only the laughter, quieter now, remained and there was ample time to absorb the beauty of the scenery.

Although we were below the Shoots, cliffs lined the river in places, interspersed with sandy banks and overhanging trees. Chatter continued with lots of ribbing about mishaps on earlier trips. In the first stretch, the river was quiet and little effort other than steering was required as we glided along with the current.

Bev moved up beside me. "How are you doing?"

"Fine, as long as it's like this." I grimaced. "Is there any fast water on this stretch?"

"Not much."

Uh-oh.

"There's a bend coming up that has a few riffles and one place after that that can be tricky, depending on how high the water is. You've canoed, though, right? So you know the basics. Follow me through. You'll be fine. Are you dried out yet?"

The warming sun had taken care of most of my t-shirt but I was regretting not removing my shorts and hanging them on the bow of the kayak.

"Not below the waist." I indicated the spray skirt that sealed the kayak up snug around my middle. "When we stop, I'll get my shorts off so they can dry."

Bev talked about the sandbar where they usually stopped for lunch—providing it wasn't under water.

"Tell me, Bev," I said. "Did Melanie's husband follow her all the way from Chicago just to spy on her or does he live around here?"

Bev glanced around to see where Melanie was. "Oh, he lives in Chicago all right. But he's obsessed about her being friends with me. I have to give Mel credit for standing up for me but it's wrecking her marriage."

"Maybe it isn't worth saving," I said.

"That's not for me to say," Bev said, and increased her paddling to pull away from me. I got the message.

The bend and the riffles didn't provide much of a challenge but had enough bumps and fast spots to make it a fun ride. The sandbar came up on the right bank shortly after that and was above water. We dragged the kayaks up and the first thing I did was remove my wet cargo shorts, all the heavier because of all the pockets. We had each brought sandwiches sealed in water-tight bags and Glynis passed out small bags of chips.

When Kurt and I had canoed, we carried all of our supplies in five-gallon buckets with water-tight lids. These buckets also served as seats when we did lunch stops but no way they would fit in a kayak, so the brown sand was the only alternative. I did have an old towel in my kayak that I could sit on and avoid coating my damp swimsuit with sand.

Conversation drifted around the group, punctuated with laughter. Glynis brought her sandwich over and perched on the end of a fallen log.

"Looks like you're doing okay." She took a big bite of ham and cheese.

I nodded. "So far. Bev said there's a little fast water coming up?" I hoped she would say something like 'I wouldn't call it fast—just a couple of riffles.' No such luck.

"There is. Sometimes we portage around it if it looks really dangerous. All depends on the river level and right now it's not real high, but it's not as low as it often is in the summer either. We'll have to wait and see."

Damn. "So, like in a canoe, you head for the 'vee' in the water?" I asked.

"Yeah, that's usually your deeper water." She wadded up her sandwich bag and stuffed it in a pocket of her shorts.

Victoria, sitting on the other end of the log, heard us talking. "One big thing to remember: if you get sideways against a rock, lean downriver. Otherwise you could flip."

I laughed. "I think once today was enough for that. I *have* seen canoes get sideways up against a logjam. It's never good."

There was a loud crack and Glynis screamed as she tumbled backward off the log.

Bev, sitting a short distance away on the sand, looked up and her face went white. "Was that a shot?" she said.

Victoria rushed to help Glynis, who looked up at her and started to giggle.

Victoria said, "No—I should have warned her that I was getting up. I think the log was rotted in the middle and her end was in the air until it broke. I'm really sorry."

Glynis waved her off and rolled over on her side, still trying to control her laughter. Victoria gave her a hand to help her up and tried to brush the sand out of her hair. I watched the color gradually return to Bev's face. A shot wouldn't be most people's first thought at a loud noise on a peaceful river bank. No one else commented on her question. The falling rock incident must have really unnerved her—more so than Victoria and I who were actually there.

Glynis continued to rub at her clothes and skin, grimacing at the abrasive grit. The others packed up their lunch remains and a few pushed off in their kayaks. By the time we had all relaunched, we were quite strung out along the river. Physically, not pharmaceutically.

"So how far to the fast water?" I asked Glynis, who was a little behind me on my right side.

"About half an hour, wouldn't you say, Victoria?"

Victoria was ahead to my left. "Sounds right," she said over her shoulder.

Glorie, who had apparently stayed off the sauce so far that day, began singing "Up a Lazy River" in a lovely, smooth contralto. We listened for a few minutes as a couple of others joined in.

"It won't be so lazy in a few minutes," Glynis commented, and then noticing the alarm on my face, added, "Just kidding. It won't be that bad."

Somehow I wasn't reassured.

CHAPTER 13

VICTORIA HAD SLOWED so that I glided alongside her and her voice broke my reverie. "You may want to put those under the spray skirt if you don't want to start all over with the drying process." She indicated my shorts that I had draped in front of me across the spray skirt.

By the time I had stowed them, I began to hear a low roar up ahead and could see a few rocks edged with foaming white water. Glynis watched the leaders intently.

"Looks like we're going through—no portage today!" She smiled at me, meant to be an encouragement.

After such a lethargic trip so far, all of a sudden we seemed headed for the rocks at warp speed. I took a deep breath and hung back to let Glynis get ahead of me.

Without a word being spoken (or yelled), the kayaks moved into a line.

As I watched, the others ahead of me followed one after another along the same route into the foaming water. Some slipped through with great grace; others detoured a little to one side or the other but managed to stay upright and headed in the right direction.

When my turn came, I aimed for the deep vee between two large boulders and only used my paddle to steer as the rushing water carried me along. I was filled with a mix of fear and exhilaration. Up ahead, I heard Glorie yell "Yeehaw! as she swung her paddle in the air. Maybe she *hadn't* stayed away from the drink and I hoped she didn't end up in it.

Up ahead, the river split in two equal streams around a massive rock and one or two took the chute to the right but most kept left. I chose the left and heard Victoria behind me holler, "Later, Gator!"

Another boulder directly ahead demanded that I turn farther to the left and had I followed instructions and turned my whole upper body with the paddle as I executed a sweep to accomplish that, I would have seen Victoria's kayak coming around the other side of the first boulder. Instead I was keeping eyes forward and when my blade caught her under the chin stopping the rhythm of my stroke, I heard a painful "Ooof!"

What happened next seemed more than warp speed. Victoria lost control of her kayak and I only caught a glimpse of the upturned bottom of her boat as she disappeared under the water before I was whisked along by the river.

"Victoria's in the water!" I yelled as I frantically scanned the area for someplace I could stop, but I was the candy on Lucy and Ethel's conveyor belt.

"Got her!" I heard someone else behind me yell. Relief, but I knew she wasn't out of the woods yet, so to speak. In what I'm sure was only a matter of minutes, I reached the end of the run.

Several kayaks milled around and some women had pulled over to the bank. It was either the practice to wait up and make sure everyone made it through safely or word of the spill had reached them.

I moved over closer to the bank and turned around just in time to see two empty kayaks come through the rapids. Bev and Glynis were close enough to grab them and pull them toward the bank.

"What happened?" Teri asked, of no one in particular.

"My fault, I'm afraid," I said. "I accidentally whacked Victoria with my paddle and she went in the water. I couldn't stop but someone yelled that they had her—I don't know who was behind her."

"It must be Melanie," Bev said. "This is her boat."

Over the roar of the rapids, we could hear shouts for help. Teri was already pulling her boat up on the bank and the rest followed. The cliffs that lined both sides of the river along the rapids ended, allowing for a wider bank on which we could pull in. But returning up the bank meant walking along a narrow ledge under the cliff and sometimes stepping in the water while clinging to a branch and hoping it was well rooted in the rock. We went single file and in a short distance, we could see Melanie on a rock. Victoria lay half on and half off the rock with her head in Melanie's lap.

Teri, in the lead, stopped and cupped her hands around her mouth. "We're here! Can she walk?"

Melanie turned to look at the row of women along the bank. The relief was visible on her face, although several treacherous-looking rocks separated by narrow streams of cold water stood between her and rescue. Victoria raised her head slightly and gave a feeble wave.

"I think so. She hit her head." Melanie held one bloody hand up for us to see.

I gulped. What had I done? I was here to save one woman and ended up hurting another. There was no time to think about it; Teri was organizing a human chain across the rocks. Everyone was pretty cautious to avoid any more accidents. The problem with any river float is that you are usually isolated at any point between the put-in and the take-out—help is not close by.

I followed Bev through the water onto the rocks. Glynis got to them first and carefully she and Melanie helped Victoria to a sitting position and then to her feet. After several false steps and near disastrous slips, they managed to get her to the next rock where Julie waited to grab her. Julie helped her on to Bev who passed her off to me.

"I am so sorry," I babbled as I helped her to the next rock and Glorie's welcoming hands. She waved my apology off but I saw the gash on the side of her head above her ear.

Melanie, Glynis, Julie, and Bev followed and we all picked our way back to the bank. The trip back down the ledge was almost as harrowing. Finally we gathered in the midst of the kayaks. Glynis guided Victoria to a stump and sat her down.

"Stay with her," she ordered Bev. "I'll be right back." Glynis rummaged inside her kayak and produced a first aid kit. While she cleaned and bandaged Victoria's head, Bev kneeled and questioned the patient, holding up fingers and checking her vision. I got my old bath towel, shook as much of the sand out as I could, and wrapped it around Victoria's shoulders.

I couldn't shake the feeling of doom no matter what action I took. Glynis finished up in short order, replacing everything in the kit. I remembered then that she was a vet's assistant and I supposed treating that kind of wound didn't vary much from animals to people.

Melanie stood shaking, wrapped in her own towel. "I think she'd have been fine if she hadn't hit her head when she ejected from her boat."

"Good thing you were behind her!" Teri said, rubbing Melanie's shoulders.

Melanie gave a little laugh. "It wasn't pretty and I couldn't pull her out without letting go of my boat."

"We caught them both," Bev said, from her crouch in front of Victoria.

"Oh, good," Melanie said, "But how are we going to get her to the take out?"

"It's pretty smooth the rest of the way," Teri said. "If she can sit up, one of us can tow her."

"I know I'm a novice, but is it possible to have one of us on each side of her so we can be right there if she faints or anything? Sort of lash them together?" I said.

Teri cocked her head. "That might work. How would you paddle?"

"Split one of the two-piece paddles — each outside person gets half," Bev said.

"Wouldn't hurt to try," Glynis said. "We can always tow her if it doesn't work."

"I think I can paddle," Victoria said in a small voice.

Melanie scoffed. "Not! You'll do what we tell you. Besides, you and I don't have paddles. Nice idea, Lynne."

Victoria shrugged and tried to give a little smile. We busied ourselves preparing for the launch. It was decided that Glynis and Teri would serve as Victoria's guides and nursemaids. Glynis split her paddle and gave half to Teri and Teri gave hers to Melanie.

We helped Victoria into her own kayak, propping her back with a couple of towels and held her boat while Bev and Teri got into theirs. Glorie produced a couple of bungee cords to help hold the boats together.

Teri said it was at least another hour or so to the take out and the mood was subdued. Victoria had had a close call and possibly a medical exam would show even more problems. I couldn't help beating myself up over my own responsibility. If I had stayed home, it wouldn't have happened. Even if I had paid closer attention to the paddling instruction, I may have avoided the accident.

I tried to take solace in the beauty around me. The good weather was holding and wispy clouds made dancing shadows on the sparkling water. There was enough of a breeze to keep the temperature comfortable and keep the bugs away.

Glorie pulled along side me.

"How are you doing?"

"Okay," I said. "I feel awful about Victoria."

"Don't. I don't mean that the way it sounds, but it's not the first accident we've had on the river and won't be the last. That is a tricky stretch. Glynis will get her to the ER when we get back. I'm sure she'll be fine."

I considered her advice and appreciated her support. It was the longest speech I had heard from her sober. "I hope so. If I had been paddling correctly, I would have seen her."

"That was only one of the problems. We should have all taken the same side. Then we would have been single file and it couldn't have happened. I'm ready for a toddy."

I hoped that wouldn't be for a while. She was a nice person to visit with. "Have you been on this trip before?"

She laughed. "Every year. I know Glynis wants me to quit drinking but that would take away the fun. I just don't see myself as a non-drinker."

I was trying to decide how to answer that when we heard a popping sound up ahead.

Glorie increased her paddling. "That sounded like a shot."

We were coming up on a bend in the river and the front of the group was out of our line of sight until we rounded the bend. Several of the kayaks were headed to the left bank, while the others milled in confusion. Bev and Melanie were the first two out of their boats on the left bank and huddled under the trees, clinging to each other. Glorie and I aimed for the same bank. Two other Sisters, Patsy and Sandy, followed us in. I glanced back over my shoulder; Glynis and Teri, with their patient between them, were making slower progress and hadn't gotten to the bend.

As we closed in on the bank, Glorie called out, "What happened?"

Melanie's voice shook. "Someone took a shot at Bev."

CHAPTER 14

GLORIE JUMPED OUT of her boat with a dexterity I wouldn't have thought she possessed. "What? Did they hit anything?"

Melanie shook her head. "Just the water. It came from over there somewhere." She pointed upriver at the opposite bank.

Bev noticed Glynis and Teri coming around the bend. She stepped to the edge of the water and waved wildly. "This way! Come over here! Hurry!"

They looked perplexed but were too far away to discuss it. Both women applied their shortened paddles diligently while keeping an eye on Victoria, who seemed to be having difficulty staying upright. As they closed in, Bev and Teri waded out in the river to help pull them in.

Any previous cautions about not standing in the river were disregarded.

After they filled Glynis in on the latest, she looked around taking a mental count. "Where's everyone else? I count five missing."

"They went toward the other bank," Melanie said. "No one knew what was happening."

What *was* happening? I was convinced that Bev was somebody's target and that it would be a factor in her death or disappearance the next night. But Naomi had never mentioned any other threats or attacks. In her mind it seemed that Bev's death was accidental and she did not question that. Surely she would have if they had been shot at. What had changed?

Glynis pulled her phone out of a water proof pouch. "So Julie's in that group on the other side?"

Melanie said, "She should be."

Glynis put her phone up to her ear while it rang. "I know she has her phone—one of her kids called at lunch."

There was quite a long wait, and then Glynis said, "Julie? Where are you guys? Which side of the river?" Listening to the answer, she grunted a couple of times and then peered across the river. I stared in the same direction and suddenly saw a figure step out from the trees downriver and wave. They must have found a cove farther down to pull their kayaks into.

Glynis ended the call and looked around our group.

"They heard the shot too and think it came from their side of the bank back up the river. They're pretty nervous about hanging around there very long. Julie said she pulled up Google Earth on her phone and the road goes along that ridge farther up river but then turns away from the river down here. So they're hoping the shooter sticks with the road. Victoria, how are you feeling?"

Victoria was leaning against a tree and looked pretty pale, but said "I'm doing better."

"Liar," Glynis said, and smiled. "Julie said they've already called the police and an ambulance and I asked them to meet us at the take-out. They're getting back on the river and will stay close to shore."

"What about us?" Bev asked. "I say we go now."

Glynis looked at the rest of the group and everyone nodded. "Our situation won't improve by staying here," Teri said.

Melanie looked especially worried. "Would it be better to join up with the rest or stay together on this side of the river?"

Bev looked back across the river. "It seems like we would be safer close to the other shore. But then we'll be very much in the open until we get over there."

"Bev, is there any possibility that what you heard was something else? A tree branch cracking or something?" Glynis said.

"I saw the bullet hit the water right after I heard the shot."

Nobody argued with that since we couldn't think of anything else that would make that noise and hit the water.

Patsy said, "Do you think it was a hunter?"

Glynis shook her head. "It shouldn't be. This part of the river is a protected area."

Patsy looked confused. She had not arrived at the campground until early that morning, so had missed the discussion after the rock incident the night before. "But—you think it's intentional?"

"It's possible. Bev has been threatened," Glynis said. "Right now we need to decide what to do next. What do you all think? Personally, I think I'd like to get back to the other side of the river."

Teri said, "I agree. Even if the shooter is still up there and is actually aiming for one of us, we'd be moving targets with the current and can kind of zig-zag our way across. I think we'd be okay."

I wasn't sure which way I would go if it was up to me so was willing to go along with the group decision. Glynis called Julie again to tell her that we would be coming up behind them soon—hopefully.

Victoria stood up, although a little wobbly. "I think I can paddle, at least a little."

Glynis started to protest, but Teri put her arm around Victoria's shoulders and said, "We could tie a tow rope from the back of my boat to the front of yours. If you can paddle enough to at least steer, we could probably move faster. Anyway until we get to the other side of the river."

THE RIVER WASN'T all that wide—after all, it wasn't the Mississippi or anything, but it seemed farther as we all scanned the wooded hillside for any sign of our attacker and still tried to avoid running into each other. Teri and Victoria were able to move a little faster than when they were three abreast with Glynis, and we made the crossing without incident. Glynis, in the lead, turned and hugged the bank and the rest followed, the relief evident in their posture. I stayed at the back since I felt responsible for Victoria's predicament and wanted to keep an eye on her.

Although we felt less vulnerable than when we were out in the open river, we continued our vigilance. I pulled up along side Victoria.

"Are you doing okay?"

She was holding herself stiffly erect but gave me a smile with an effort and a slight nod. "I'll be glad to lay down."

"How much farther is it to the take out, do you remember?"

"Hard to say exactly. I've done this stretch twice before, but I remember more about the first half than this part. I think there's an old falling-down barn coming up and then the take-out is just past that."

"Good, " I said. "I can't tell you how sorry I am. What a klutz!"

"Please don't worry about it." She was obviously tired and rested her paddle in front of her but then took a slight jolt as the rope connecting her to Teri tightened up. "Oops. Now we now what a 'slacker' is."

"Are you okay?" Teri called back.

"Yeah—my bad. Here comes that barn!" She pointed ahead.

I'm not sure I could have identified it as a barn had I been alone. A stone foundation was all that stood and part of that had tumbled, leaving gaps. It more closely resembled a Roman ruin. Piles of weathered boards, partially covered by vines and grass, scattered around the foundation like jackstraws. But it made an appealing picture.

However, I hadn't brought a camera on this trip. The changed technology in cameras and phones would raise questions and I wasn't sure the photos would survive time travel. It was an interesting question but one I hadn't yet explored. Besides, we had more urgent concerns on our minds than photos and we continued our unvaried and rhythmic paddling.

Relief at the sight of the other kayaks dragged up on the bank swept over all of us, and there were a few cheers.

The Sisters who had already landed came forward to pull us in. Julie and another woman helped Victoria out of her boat and they were quickly replaced by two EMTs who had emerged from the flashing ambulance parked near the ramp. They guided her to and helped her onto a gurney.

One EMT, a middle aged man, took off the bandage Glynis had devised and began to clean the cut on Victoria's head while the other, a young woman, looked in her eyes with a direct ophthalmoscope. The rest of us helped the cute young man from the rental outfit identify the boats belonging to them, and one by one he hefted them on to the trailer rack, checking each one off. Glynis and Bev moved toward a sheriff's deputy getting out of his car.

I helped Teri reload her kayak and our supplies into her truck.

"I told the EMTs that I would come to the clinic, hopefully to bring Victoria back. They gave me directions. I just need to let Glynis know," she said, when we finished.

"I'll go with you if you don't mind."

"Love to have you."

We headed over to Glynis, Bev, and the deputy.

"So you think this person was shooting *at* you?" The deputy closed his notebook and stuck it back in his pocket. He raised one eyebrow at Bev. "Does that happen a lot?"

Bev spoke quietly, as if she didn't expect to be believed. "Look. I reported some shady dealings at a drug company that I worked for. Now they're out to get me."

"You've been shot at before?" The eyebrow went higher.

"No. Not that I know of. There was the sound of a shot and then something hit the water right in front of my kayak."

"But it *could* have been a breaking branch and maybe a fish jumping at the same time?" The deputy appeared to be holding back a smile.

"I'm pretty sure it wasn't," Bev said. She held the deputy's stare and her face got red.

"Well, we'll do what we can but it's a big area to cover and there's not much of anyone up on that hill to be a witness. I'll be in touch," the deputy said, and returned to his car.

"I won't hold my breath," Glynis said, when he was out of earshot.

"Ma'am?" The young man from the boat rental outfit was standing behind her with a clipboard.

"Yes, sorry about that. Did you get all of your boats?" She took the clipboard from him and signed where he had marked an 'X.'

"Sure did. Sounds like you had an exciting float. Ambulance, police—" He smirked a little, but caught himself when Glynis frowned.

"Um, sorry—didn't mean it the way it sounded. Say, did that guy find you?"

"What *guy*?" Glynis gave him back the clipboard and focused on him intently.

"A guy came to the office and asked where you ladies would be taking out. It seemed pretty urgent."

"And you told him? What was his name? What did he look like?"

Rental guy realized he was only getting in deeper. "Uh, Callie, the receptionist did. It sounded important, I guess. I don't think they got his name." He held up his hands. "I wasn't there."

"Well, maybe *that guy* is why we needed to call the ambulance and the police," Glynis said.

The kid stared at her, confused. The rest of us stood around and tried to hide our smiles at the young man's discomfort.

"Tell Callie we'll be talking to her...or the police will. This *guy* may have made an attempt on someone's life. Thank you."

Judging from the shock on the young man's face, the import of the police presence hadn't registered until Glynis' last words.

"Un, yeah, sure will." He made a fast exit.

Glynis stood for a moment shaking her head and then turned toward her truck.

"Glynis?" Teri said. "Lynne and I are going to the clinic to see what they say about Victoria. We hope we'll be able to bring her back to the campground."

"Great! Let us know if she needs anything." I must have had a pretty hangdog look, because she glanced at me and said, "Don't beat yourself up. It was an accident and accidents happen."

"Thanks," I said, but I wasn't sure I could take her

words to heart. Not only did my carelessness cause Victoria's injuries, but I couldn't help wondering if stopping to rescue her and treat the gash on her had allowed someone time to get in place to take a shot at Bev, if indeed she was the target. I didn't know how else to explain the apparent change in events from Melanie's account.

CHAPTER

15

WE BOUNCED OVER the back roads to the highway leading to Gustafson, where the clinic was located.

"Who do you think this 'guy' is that the rental kid was talking about?" I asked Teri, when we got to the smoother road.

"Beats me—unless it's Melanie's husband."

"Even if he doesn't like Melanie hanging out with Bev—I mean, isn't shooting her a little extreme?"

"I get the impression he is pretty extreme."

I still didn't get it. "Bev seems to think it has to do with the whistle blowing."

Teri shrugged. "Apparently that's why Melanie's husband doesn't like Bev—because of what she did to a couple of his buddies. But maybe there *wasn't* a shot." She glanced sideways at me, gauging my reaction.

I was confused. Everyone in the group had seemed to accept Bev's version of the events except the deputy, but now Teri seemed to have her doubts.

"Maybe not," I conceded. "I'm not sure *I* could swear to something that happened that fast."

"Well, I hope Glynis finds out something at the rental place," she said, and we retreated into our own thoughts for the rest of the ride.

THE CLINIC WAS NEW, small, and according to the sign, a satellite of an area hospital. We told the receptionist who we were there for and she suggested we take a seat in the waiting area and she would call us.

After only fifteen minutes or so, a nurse came out, spoke to the receptionist, and motioned us over. There wasn't an emergency room per se, so we were ushered back to an examining room. Victoria sat on the edge of a table, her face a little brighter than it had been. A large white patch covered the gash above her ear. Her dark curly hair had been cut and shaved away around the area. A tall, thin woman in a white coat turned when we entered and smiled.

"How is she?" Teri asked.

The doctor eyed our getups and wild hair. "I assume you were with her when this happened?"

"I'm afraid it was my fault," I said. "Accidentally, of course. I caught her with my paddle."

Victoria shook her head slowly. "Could have happened to anyone."

"Well, the good news is that she doesn't have a concussion."

"But there's bad news too," Victoria said.

"What?" Teri and I said in unison.

Victoria grinned at us. "I'm not going to be able to wear my new cowboy hat to the cowgirl prom tomorrow night."

Teri breathed a visible sigh of relief. "You'll just have to wear it on your back. It worked for Dale Evans."

The night before, there had been a long discussion about the cowgirl 'prom', a popular Sisters activity, planned for Saturday night,. A local country western trio was scheduled to play, everyone would dress outrageously, there would be a BBQ supper, drinks and dancing for those who chose. However, I suspected the event would never take place on this weekend so I didn't worry about Victoria's new hat.

Victoria slid off the examining table and we helped her out to the truck. I took the smaller crew seat in the back so that she could ride in the passenger seat up front.

By the time we were back in the campground, the rest of the group had gathered at Glynis' camper and were loudly reviewing the events of the day. Glynis was emptying her truck and I helped her. I took the opportunity to ask her if she had stopped at the rental office.

"Yes, I did. Melanie went with me because she suspected that her husband was still checking up on her. But she showed Callie — their Girl Friday — a photo of her husband and Callie said it wasn't him. Had a snake tattooed on his arm, she said."

"Which arm?" I asked, because it seemed an obvious question.

Glynis gave a wry smirk. "She couldn't remember. Regardless, I want everyone to stay in a group tonight."

Victoria received everyone's sympathetic and encouraging words and looked pretty beat.

"You look like you need a nap. Can I walk you to your camper?" I said.

She gingerly pushed her hair back. "Sounds great but I really need a shower first. Would you mind going with me?"

"Only if I can grab one too. The river didn't look dirty but I feel like I'm covered with scum. I'll run up and get my stuff and Jeep, pick you up and we'll get your things."

"Great!" She leaned back in her chair. "I can rest up."

Teri asked to join us — I think we were all a little concerned that Victoria might pass out in the shower and didn't want her left alone. By the time I returned with the Jeep, she appeared to be almost nodding off. But there is nothing so appealing when you are sweaty and dirty as a shower and fresh clothes. When I touched her shoulder, she sat up and brightened.

"I'm ready!" We stopped at her camper to get her things and Teri ran across the road to her own camper.

Victoria's vintage camper was named "Her Majesty" and the sides were painted with the Union Jack. The famous profile silhouette of Queen Victoria was painted alongside the rear window and above in fancy script were the words, "We are easily amused." Inside, the windows and furnishings dripped with lace, fringe, wine colored velvet and gold embellishments.

"This is stunning," I said. "Doesn't it require a lot of upkeep?"

"Not really." She ran her hand over the snowy white damask tablecloth on the dinette. The supporting leg in the center of the table appeared to be ornately carved wood and the bench cushions were covered in velvet edged with gold braid. A crystal bowl in the center of the table held large dark red cabbage roses. Satin pillows in dark blue and red nestled in the corners.

"Everything is fake," she explained with a grin. "The fabrics are washable polyester and the wood, gold trim, and glassware is actually plastic."

"You fooled me. It looks wonderful."

Once back in the Jeep, I headed toward the shower house which was near the entrance of the campground. As I turned into a parking place at the front, Teri said, "Maybe the deputy took us more seriously than we thought." She pointed to the entrance where a patrol car sat.

"Good," I said, "But I can't imagine that they have the personnel to keep that up very long."

"It won't stop anyone from walking in but maybe it'll make 'em think twice," Victoria said.

We trooped into the shower house where a couple of other Sisters were already availing themselves of the facilities. We had Victoria take the only empty stall while we waited on the bench. By the time we all finished and gushed about the wonderful feeling of clean, it was mid-afternoon.

Teri and I opted to rest in reclining lawn chairs outside Victoria's camper while she napped, in case she needed anything.

Glynis walked over to check on things. She, Melanie and Bev were doing some cast iron cooking for the evening's supper. They insisted they had everything under control and we should just be available for Victoria.

"There's a deputy stationed at the main gate," Teri told her.

"I requested that," Glynis said. "It's probably only for today, but I thought at least we could relax a little. The Sheriff's department was pretty reluctant."

Teri nodded. "I'm not surprised. Unless they find another witness, they only have our word that it happened. Any bullets are at the bottom of the river."

"Well, no outsiders will be allowed into the campground tonight, including Melanie's husband. So we can just enjoy the evening. I'd better get back — Bev will be giving me demerits."

Teri asked me about my family and I gave her the Reader's Digest version. She commiserated with me over the thrills and agonies of raising a teenaged girl.

"I have two daughters and they're great. But they're also in their thirties, now. My son Jimmy, as I told you last night, is disabled and still lives at home and really can't be left on his own, so my younger daughter Liz is staying at the house this weekend. They're both really good about that. But I tried to give them away a number of times when they were in their teens." She laughed.

"So true," I said.

She hoisted herself out of her chair and stretched. "I'm going to go get ready for supper. I couldn't decide between two outfits for the prom tomorrow night so I brought 'em both and I'm wearing one tonight."

"I'm afraid I'll be the sore thumb," I said and indicated my outfit. "This is it."

She waved off my comment. "Not everyone dresses up. This is one group you can't be out of place no matter what you wear."

SHE WAS RIGHT. When Victoria got up from her rest, she changed into a turquoise shirt festooned with silver and beads and a tie-died full skirt, finished off with cowboy boots.

"Wow!" I said. "Would the Queen approve?"

"You know, I think she would."

"I would go change but I didn't bring anything along that would even be in the running with that outfit."

"Why would you? You had no idea you would be in the company of such snazzy women. Want to borrow something?"

"No, thanks." I put on a sad face. "I don't like sympathy wardrobes. You look like you are feeling quite a bit better."

"I am—still a dull ache in my head, but *much* better than it was."

CHAPTER 16

SISTERS WERE GATHERING. As predicted, some sported all of their plumage and some dressed in typical, but clean, camping clothes. Vintage and western wear stores must love to see these ladies coming. Even the cooks were split. Bev wore khaki slacks and a blue oxford cloth shirt while Glynis had on a yellow shirtwaist over full petticoats, protected by a a red and white checked gathered apron. I didn't see Melanie at first until I went to the bar table to pour a glass of wine. She stood around the corner from the camper in the road talking to the owner of the maroon BMW—her husband, Tabor.

It didn't look like the confrontation I would have expected. Melanie hugged herself and appeared to be crying, while Tabor gently rested a hand on her shoulder and seemed to be comforting her. I normally shy away from private moments but remembered my mission and threw courtesy to the wind.

Carrying my wine glass, I strolled toward them.

"Melanie? Is everything all right?"

She looked up and wiped her eyes with her hand.

"This is my husband, Tabor," she said when I got closer. "It's our son, Justin. Tabor just got him committed to rehab."

I remembered Naomi/Melanie telling me about her son and his problem with pain relievers after a tennis injury. Of course, this Melanie didn't know I knew that.

"Oh, I'm sorry. I mean, that's a good thing, right?" I should shut up.

She gave a slight nod. "It's a relief, yes."

Tabor pretty much ignored me. "I'll leave now. But I didn't want to tell you over the phone. Take care."

He sounded sincere—sort of. But I couldn't shake the image I had built up of him.

As he pulled away, Melanie and I walked back around the trailer to the group. As we did, I said, "Nice of him to come all this way to tell you."

"What? Well, he's fishing with some buddies across the river in Illinois. Yeah, I guess."

"What kind of rehab?"

"Prescription drugs. He got hooked after a tennis injury to his shoulder. He used to be a nice kid."

Used to be? Pretty strong condemnation from a mother. I didn't detect much hope in her voice.

"How old is he?"

"Twenty-four. He's been in rehab before and it didn't do much good."

"Umm, I think I've read that the more times they go through that, the better the chances of success."

"Hey, girls! Grab a plate," Teri called as we came around the corner. Sisters were lining up at a table where Bev and Glynis dished up bowls of a rice, sausage and sweet potato mixture and large wedges of cornbread slathered with butter. There were also bowls of fruit and coleslaw.

"Looks fantastic," I said to Bev as I took my plate. She nodded and looked sideways at Melanie, who was behind me. She seemed to be searching for something on Melanie's face, but Melanie was turned aside visiting with someone else. I continued through the line.

I told Glynis, "You're only missing a string of pearls."

"I know. I have some but I couldn't find them!" She shaped the collar of her shirtwaist and grinned.

The line moved along and we found seats in lawn chairs under the awning. Melanie saved a place next to her for Bev, who joined us after the line was through.

"What was Tabor here for, Mel?" she said when she sat down.

Melanie sighed. "It's Justin. He's in rehab again."

Bev shook her head. "That hasn't helped much in the past, has it?"

"Lynne thinks the more times he goes through it, the more effective it is," Melanie said, but I could tell she wasn't buying it.

"Let me work with him," Bev said. "I've had some training — maybe he would connect better with someone he knows."

"Thanks for the offer but Tabor has probably warped his mind toward you. I don't hold out much hope."

Bev patted her arm. "Let's talk about it after we get home and we can make a plan."

Melanie didn't answer so I said, "This food is excellent. I'd ask for the recipe, but I'm not much of a cook."

"It's easy peasy," Bev said. "I can tell you how."

"Thanks. Let's do it later. I would definitely need to take notes."

We concentrated on the food while chatter went on around us. It gave me a chance to think. Maybe Tabor wasn't such a bad egg after all. At least he had a reason for being here. I took my plate to the trash and stopped to talk to Victoria.

"How are you getting along?"

"Really well, I think. I'm tired but we probably all are." She indicated the empty chair next to her. "Sit"

I sat. "Great supper," I said.

"For sure. Some of the gals are talking about going to a nearby country bar. I think I'm up for it for a little while. You?"

I looked at her in surprise and laughed. "I lead a pretty quiet life at home. I'm not sure I can keep up with this group."

"Oh, come on—you're younger than me!"

"Yeah, but—"

"No yeah buts. They're going in about an hour—gives our suppers plenty of time to settle. Can you drive?" She noticed my expression and added, "That's not why I asked you to go, honest. I just like your Jeep."

"Your taste is questionable. It's pretty old, but I would be glad to drive."

"What year is it?"

"2000."

"That's not bad—that's only five years."

Whoops. I forgot that my Jeep wasn't fifteen years old in 2005. "Whatever. I don't think I want to ride with someone who has a head injury anyway, you know?" I grinned at her and we agreed on a departure time. Teri said she would like to hitch a ride too.

THE BAR WAS one of those found in almost every non-dry county in America. It could be perfect for an archeological study. Places in the floor showed evidence of several succeeding updates of linoleum and tile, as well as the original wood. A bulletin board by the door also displayed layers and layers of crucial announcements, including a number of sale ads. I wondered if the ad for the blue Dodge on one of the top sheets maybe had earlier ads underneath from previous sales.

I was sure the odors of stale smoke and beer were probably embedded in the walls. The noise was deafening as voices and music ricocheted off the hard surfaces. I regretted my decision to come but could hardly strand Victoria and Teri so took a seat with the group around a sticky table. Glynis and Bev got a couple of pitchers of beer and glasses.

I scanned the crowd. It looked like mostly locals with lots of baseball caps sporting seed corn or sports logos. One table near the back stuck out like the proverbial sore thumb. Three men wore shirts with buttons and no hats. Two of them were very focused on our table, but that could have been because of the attire of some of our group—not typical for even this place. Actually, we were getting stares from several other tables as well.

Bev noticed me staring and turned around to see what I was looking at. She turned immediately back, her face infused with anger.

"What is it?" I tried to communicate over the din.

She shook her head. "Later!" she yelled back.

It was so difficult to talk and it wasn't long before I noticed Victoria beginning to droop as the adrenaline wore off. I nudged her.

"Do you want to leave?" I practically yelled in her ear.

"I'm fine," she said without conviction.

"Seriously," I said, "this isn't for me."

Teri leaned over. "You guys thinking about leaving? I'm ready if you are."

In the end the whole group exited, sucking in the fresh outside air and relishing the quieter sounds of the night. We felt relief as the bar door slammed and effectively muffled the raucous bar noise.

"Wow!" Teri said. "Maybe I'm getting too old too."

"Maybe we're getting smarter," I said.

THE ATMOSPHERE IN the bar must have felt pretty oppressive to everyone in the group because as we piled out of the vehicles back at the campground, we sounded like school kids let out for summer vacation. Glynis stoked up the fire, chairs were rearranged and drinks replenished.

"I think I'll turn in," Victoria said as she gingerly let herself down from the Jeep.

"I'll walk you back. We wouldn't want you to pass out on the road."

"Really, Lynne — it's not necessary — "

"Just let me do it because it makes me feel better," I said. "Don't argue with me."

After I returned from seeing her tucked safely inside the 'Queen,' I walked over to Bev, who was laughing about something with Julie.

"Did you know those guys at the back table at the bar? They didn't look like they were local."

The smile disappeared. She brushed her hair back from her face. "They might be following me."

"Have you seen them before?"

"No, not them specifically. But they look like the type of guys who follow me sometimes. Maybe I'm just crazy."

I had the feeling that last statement was a disclaimer meant to elicit 'Of course, you're not' responses. I didn't say anything.

FOR THE NEXT HOUR, I enjoyed the conversation of the women and listening to their camping experiences. Then they began to say their goodnights and drift off toward their respective campers and tents. I was deciding to join them when Teri and I got into a political discussion. Her point of view intrigued me and we were in the midst of a lively discussion about welfare when a scream rent the night quiet.

It came from closer to the river where several of the Sisters had tents. Those of us still around the fire jumped up and headed that way.

Bev stood facing her tent, her hand to her chest, looking both frightened and embarrassed.

Teri got there first. "What is it?"

Bev sucked in a deep breath and pointed at her tent. "A snake—I think it's a copperhead—inside my tent."

Glynis pulled out her phone. "I'll call the ranger. Was your door zipped?"

"Yes!" Bev was very firm. "I hate snakes and never leave without making sure all the openings are sealed."

The unzipped door now draped off to the side. The inside was partially lit with diffused light.

"I dropped my flashlight when I saw it," Bev explained.

Teri looked around at the other six or seven women. "Anyone else have a flashlight?" Glorie pulled one out of her pocket, looked as if she was surprised to find it, and handed it to Teri.

Glynis put her phone away and reported that the ranger was on his way, while Teri cautiously moved to where she could shine the light directly in the door. In the limited scope of the doorway, we could see piles on the floor—a sleeping bag perhaps and some clothes.

"Something moved!" Glorie pointed, her eyes wide.

Bev nodded. "By the sleeping bag? I saw that!"

"No, by the clothes…" Glorie said.

Someone else thought they saw the edge of the tent wiggle, and it was with great relief that I saw the ranger pull up in his truck. He and a young woman got out wearing heavy gloves and carrying long sticks. Bev pointed in the open tent and we all backed up. The woman bent to enter the tent with the pole in one hand and a flashlight held overhead. The man remained outside by the door, ready to catch any escapees. We backed up some more.

We milled around, exchanging a little snake humor in an effort to calm our nerves until the woman emerged, shaking her head.

"Have you been watching the tent the whole time?" she asked.

Bev was flustered. "Yes — I think so — I mean, I ran out of the tent and started screaming, um — " She paused and looked around.

Julie stepped forward. "I got here first. You were over there and I don't think you were facing the tent then."

"Well, it must have gotten out then," the ranger said. "Maybe you'd rather sleep somewhere else tonight to be sure?"

"She'll be staying with me," Melanie said, and then turned to Bev. "No arguments."

"Good idea," said the ranger. "How about if I help you find what you need out of your tent and then we'll zip it up for the night? I'll check it again in the morning."

Bev let out a deep breath. "That would be great!" In spite of her enthusiasm for that plan, she followed the ranger into the tent tentatively. Melanie stood by to take the clothes and bedding Bev handed out the door — after the ranger checked each item.

After the door was securely zipped, I helped them carry Bev's things up to Melanie's trailer. Like mine, the interior was wood but the turquoise color on the exterior was repeated in the appliances, sink and beachy curtains.

"This is great, Mel!"

"Thanks," she said, beaming. "I love it, and since Tabor doesn't want to camp, it's great for just me." She looked at Bev. "Or me and Bev," she added hastily, when she saw Bev's face. "The dinette makes into a bed."

"Mine, too," I said. "Well, I don't know about you guys but I think it's been a rather full day and I'm ready for *my* bed, for sure, so I'll say good night."

They didn't try and dissuade me; if anything they looked more ready to crash than I did.

CHAPTER 17

I HAD INTENDED to try and sort out the day's events before I went to sleep but don't remember even getting into bed. Obviously, I had, so I lay there in the morning, thinking. Always a scary prospect.

I had lots of questions. Bev was an enigma to me. So far, in twenty-four hours, she seemed to be the target of a falling rock, a sniper, and a hidden snake. But the rock was dropped on Victoria and me, not everyone was convinced that the sound on the river was a shot—including law enforcement—and no one except Bev saw the snake. She thought the log breaking on the sandbar was a shot and showed fear at the sight of the strangers in the bar. Something didn't ring true and yet her story was not far-fetched. She had defied a major corporation and could very well be under a threat.

Then there was Melanie's husband, Tabor. My impression of him from my previous research and first experiences this weekend was that he was a low-down scumbag, but it was only an impression. Since he had made a trip over to break the news to Melanie about their son in person, maybe he wasn't so bad.

Even more crucial to me was how I might be affecting the time line. My goal had been to simply keep Bev safe from the flash flood and not change anything else. But it appeared I had already done just that. If Bev had been shot at originally, Melanie surely would have suspected that Bev's disappearance was not accidental and would have mentioned it. I had to assume that the delay I caused by injuring Victoria somehow had created that opportunity.

And if I was going to keep Bev safe from the flood, how would I do that? It occurred to me that there was another woman who disappeared with Bev, but I didn't remember who that was. It must have been another one of the tenters. I knew Patsy was in a tent but couldn't remember who else. I wondered if the snake incident could be used to get all of the tenters away from the river tonight. Maybe I could report a snake sighting?

I looked at my little vintage windup alarm clock. It was 8:00 a.m. already and Teri was serving breakfast at 8:30. She had promised homemade cinnamon rolls. I wondered if excess calories that I put away while time traveling stuck around when I returned home. I guessed I would find out. The forecast for the day was a little cooler and a shopping trip to a nearby antique mecca was planned for the morning, so I donned jeans, a white loose shirt and sandals. In an effort to get into the cowgirl spirit, I tied my hair back with a bandana.

The group at Teri's trailer appeared completely revitalized after a night's sleep. Teri was cooking an omelet in a large electric skillet and motioned me toward the coffee pot.

"What can I do?" I asked, sipping the dark roast brew.

"This is ready. If you don't mind, go in my camper and bring out the tray of bacon from the oven—it's on warm."

We had barely gotten perched in lawn chairs balancing our plates and I was in ecstasy over the fragrance, texture, and taste of my first bite of cinnamon roll, when Bev and the woman ranger came up the road. Melanie sat forward in her chair.

"Any sign of anything?" she called out to them.

Bev shook her head and smiled. "Looks clear," she called.

"Come have some breakfast," Teri said.

Bev held up a towel bundle. "I'm going to go grab a shower first."

"I'll save you a roll!" Teri called after her.

THE TOWN OF CHEVY'S FORD showed off its Victorian main street with fancy paint jobs, striped awnings, vintage looking street lights with hanging baskets of red and purple petunias, and brightly painted benches in front of the stores.

Clever store names beckoned from elaborate overhead signs. My favorite was The Time Traveler, but I didn't mention why. We parked in a public parking lot on a side street and I gained new respect for the Sisters as shoppers when they unfolded wheeled shopping carts and displayed flamboyant shopping bags.

"I feel woefully underprepared," I told Glorie, as she slung a woven multi-colored Mexican bag over her shoulder.

"I have another — do you want it?"

"I don't think so — I'm not much of a shopper," I said. Actually I wasn't sure whether I could take anything back to my time with me. We headed down the street, hitting the first store as a group and then splintering off into smaller bunches as different stores struck our fancy.

Sandy, a short bubbly blond, was looking for things to add to her cowgirl-themed camper and was ecstatic about a cache of Dale Evans memorabilia in one shop. One Sister, whose name I can't remember, was collecting old handkerchiefs to make a quilt for her trailer. Patsy was delighted with a battered Firetime marshmallows advertising sign. And so on.

I had been honest with Glorie—I really am not much of a shopper, but discovered I loved helping to look for things the others were searching for.

Teri and I were in one junk shop sorting through old silverware. She was looking for more forks although not any particular pattern so I tried to select some I thought she might like.

"Oooh, love that one—and that, but not that flowered one." She picked out a couple of others, and then changed the subject. "What do you think about Bev? Do you think someone's really trying to hurt—or kill—her?"

I thought about playing dumb but shrugged. "I don't know. No one else seems to actually have seen the same thing. Do you know her very well?"

"I've been to several events with her—four or five—but she's kind of hard to get close to."

"I could see that. She seems close to Melanie."

"They've been friends for a long time," she said, as she headed to the cash register with her finds. Adding her purchases to her shopping bag, she returned to the subject. "I don't know—sometimes I think she's just trying to get sympathy. But that's probably not fair."

Outside we joined a group of Sisters in front of an old fashioned five and dime. Glynis was displaying a straw cowboy hat and a handful of feathers and rhinestones that she planned to decorate it with. Bev and Melanie came out of the store next door, laughing and looking more relaxed than I had seen them all weekend.

"Is it time for lunch, yet?" Bev asked.

"There's an Irish pub down the block," Glorie said.

Glynis snorted. "You're only interested in the pub part."

Glorie tossed her head and grinned. "What of it? I'm honest." She led the way.

Inside the dark, rustic-looking bar, we found two tables and pushed them together. It was a little early for lunch and there was not much of a crowd yet.

"Didn't we just eat breakfast?" Victoria said, to no one in particular.

"Shopping saps the strength," Teri said as she opened the menu. Behind the bar, a young woman in jeans and a peasant blouse with a white towel wrapped around her middle started over to wait on us. One of the men at the bar said something to her that she apparently found a little offensive. She looked at him a moment and continued toward us.

"What can I help you ladies with today?" She took a quick glance over her shoulder at the man at the bar. He was still watching her and he looked familiar but I couldn't figure out why.

We ordered and when we finished, the waitress said, "Do you mind if I ask why some of you are...dressed up?"

Glynis explained the Sisters and what they did.

"That is awesome!" the waitress said. "Well, I'll get these orders up." When she returned to the bar, she only gave curt acknowledgement to the man who seemed interested in us. He kept trying to get a rise out of her but she went about turning in our order to a disembodied hand through a serving window.

Just then another woman entered the bar, came up behind him, and gave him a kiss on the cheek. He turned on his stool and broke into a big grin. She held up two big shopping bags for his inspection, which didn't interest him much. He said something and nodded toward us. She turned and then I realized where I had seen them. They were one of the couples I had met in the campground the first night—the guy who had been suspicious of the large group of women—Gary, I think. She nodded at me, and he got off his stool, heading toward us with his glass of beer. His wife put a hand on his arm but he shook it off.

"Hey, ladies, nice day, huh? Decided to get away from camp for a little shopping?"

Teri took the lead. "We did. Have we met, Mr. — ?"

"Jes' call me Gary. We're out at the campground, too. Sounds like you gals have had some troubles—snakes and stuff?" He could hardly keep the glee out of his voice.

His wife joined him. "Gary, let's go order some lunch and leave these women alone." She looked at me apologetically.

"Sure, honey—I thought maybe they needed a man's help. We're in site #15 down by the river if you need anything." He grinned as if he was sure we were just waiting to jump on his offer. The waitress edged by him with a large tray of food and started calling out the orders. Gary's wife ushered him away, and the waitress rolled her eyes.

"What a creep," Victoria said.

"I met them the other night on my way back to my camper. It obviously bothered him then that women could survive on their own." I took a basket of shrimp and fries off the tray.

"Fortunately, we don't run into that too often," Glynis said. "Most of the men have been pretty supportive."

"I'm sorry that he bothered you," the waitress said. "He's been asking about you since you came in."

Teri waved her apology away. "Not your fault. This looks great!" She picked up a juicy looking Reuben and took a big bite. "Excellent," she said, around a full mouth. Discussion switched to the morning's purchases and treasures passed up.

As we headed back toward the campground, I noticed the sky clouding up. Teri, riding with me, looked at the weather forecast on her phone.

"Bummer," she said. "This could literally put a damper on the cowgirl prom."

And that ain't all, I thought, but didn't say it.

Glynis sat forward from the back. "I'm going to talk to the rangers about using the enclosed shelter. I'm sure we can, if it's not already reserved."

"Where is the shelter?" I asked. "I don't think I've seen that."

"It's farther upriver right on the bank. There's some trees between it and the campground so you can't see it."

Great. That would put the whole group in harm's way. I wished fervently that I had asked Melanie/Naomi more details about the weekend. Did they have the prom, and if so, where? At what time did the flood hit? Once again, I realized I hadn't thought this through or done enough research.

"Do they ever have flash flooding along here? There might be cause for concern if there's going to be heavy rains. Some of those campsites are pretty close to the river." I said this as if I had just thought of it.

"We've had rain before and never had a problem," Glynis said. "We should get a warning if they think there's even a chance."

Should being the operative word.

I STOOD OUTSIDE my camper and surveyed the hillside down to the river. I could see Bev's tent along with several others close to the bank. Melanie's and Teri's trailers were up at the next level. Glynis and Victoria were at the tent level along with several larger trailers and a motorhome. Maybe one of them belonged to Gary the Creep and his wife. The roof of the shelter that Glynis hoped to reserve showed above the trees.

If only I had checked on the time that flash flood hit

here. I didn't bring my laptop for a number of reasons but I should be able to get online and check a forecast at the local library. I decided I wouldn't mention my plan to anyone else or someone might want to go along.

It was only about ten minutes back into town and I stopped at the first gas station to get directions to the library. It occupied a converted storefront at the end of main street. Inside, the front was dedicated to childrens' books with low, bright-colored tables and chairs. A young man behind a desk in the center looked up from a stack of books.

"May I help you?"

"Do you have a public computer with internet access?"

He smiled. "We do. Several." He pointed at a small glassed in cubicle at the back of the room. When I started that way, he said, "I need to have you sign in first, though." He turned an open spiral notebook around to face me. I signed my name, looked at my watch, and added the time and the date.

As I turned the notebook back to him and straightened, he added, almost apologetically, "I also need to see a photo ID."

That stopped me. Would he check the date on my driver's license? It was out of state so would probably be unfamiliar to him. I had credit cards but nothing else with a photo. I slowly got out my license and put my thumb over the date. I pretended my hesitation was embarrassment over my photo—it didn't require much acting.

He glanced at the picture, suppressed a smile, and nodded permission.

I was pretty sure no one had ever gone through such stress to find out a weather forecast.

I went back to the cubicle. There were six bulky monitors with keyboards and tower hard drives on a counter that went around three sides of the room. Young teenagers played video games at two of them and the rest were available. I sat down at the end one.

It took some doing, and the slowness of the ten-year-old (to me) technology was frustrating, but I was finally able to find a local weather radar, along with an hourly forecast. Rain would begin about 7:00 in the evening. There were currently no flash flood watches or warnings. A large red and yellow blob was moving down from the northwest but had a ways to go. It looked like the flood would hit during the night—much more dangerous when people were asleep.

CHAPTER 18

BACK AT THE CAMPGROUND, I parked again and walked down to Glynis' camper. She was excited and loading boxes in her truck.

"The shelter is available! Want to help me decorate?"

"Uh, sure. I don't have to do anything creative, do I?"

She threw back her head and laughed. "No, Teri and I planned it all out. More hands will make putting it up go faster."

"Okay," I said. "I can be a grunt."

We climbed in her truck and drove to the shelter. Teri was already there and helped carry boxes in. Glynis designated one corner for the band, after checking to make sure there were outlets available.

"There's three bales of straw near the front of my truck bed. Can you girls get those?"

I shook my head. "Packing your truck must be a real challenge."

She smiled. "Practice."

Teri and I arranged the straw in the corner for the band—decoration and seating. Glynis directed the arrangement of tables around the walls. We unpacked centerpieces of artificial daisies in canning jars and placed them on bandanas on each table. Glynis got a suitcase out of the back seat of her truck. She opened it on one of the tables to reveal a heap of old clothes.

"What are those for?" I asked.

She pulled out a white lace camisole and held it up. "Laundry," she said. Teri was hanging rope along the walls and they added the clothes with clothes pins: more camisoles, bib overalls, calico skirts, white bloomers, long underwear, stockings, and flannel shirts.

"Very clever," I said. I helped hang more items until we had them around every wall.

"We'll set the food table over here." Glynis point to the wall opposite the corner for the band. "Patsy and Julie are bringing roasters to keep the BBQ warm." She spread a red-checked vinyl table cloth over one of the tables and we moved it to the chosen place. Teri brought in a large box containing a variety of lanterns and we placed at least one on each table.

Glynis stood back to assess the result. "What do you think?"

"It looks terrific!" Teri said.

Glynis looked at her watch. "I need to go get ready." She waggled her eyebrows. "We start at 5:00. Maybe the rain will hold off."

As the appointed time neared, I put on a clean denim shirt with my jeans and headed down to Teri's camper. She came to the door in a red-checked shirt with white piping, a fringed red skirt and cowboy boots.

"Wow!" I said. "Look at you. Queen of the Cowgirls."

"Right. Come on in."

This was my first chance to really look around Teri's Serro Scotty trailer. "Wow, again." I looked around. "This is really cute." The ceiling was pressed copper, the walls white with some beadboard paneling, and the fabrics a mix of teal, brown and white plaid, teal, brown, and yellow paisley, and teal and white polka dots. Yellow and white tiles covered the floor.

"My son and I did it. He's very talented when he can focus. We camp in it together quite a bit and he enjoys it. I'll finish and we'll see if Victoria's ready."

"I know it isn't far," I said, "but I drove so we could give her a ride."

"Great." She disappeared into the tiny bathroom and returned fluffing her hair. "Let's saddle up."

Victoria was sitting outside waiting for us. I had to laugh at how she had camouflaged the bandage on her head. She had pulled her dark, curly hair to the other

147

side and covered the bandage with a huge red silk rose right above her ear. A white peasant blouse, red full skirt and black embroidered shawl completed her outfit.

"Doesn't look like Queen Vicky to me," I said.

Victoria smiled demurely. "She had a private side no one knew about."

"Except you," Teri said.

"Except me."

"So you decided to forego your new cowboy hat," I said.

"Yup. There'll be another time."

IN THE SHELTER, the lanterns had been lit and the sound of laughter filtered out into the late afternoon shadows. The trio wasn't set to start until after supper so a guitar CD played in the background. Clusters of Sisters milled around admiring the decorations and eying the rapidly filling buffet table. Bev motioned us over. She was all in black: cowboy hat, shirt, jeans, and boots.

"If you'd go outside and lean against the wall, everyone would think you were one of those yard ornaments," Teri said.

Bev nodded. "A new career, perhaps?"

Victoria said, "I don't think it pays very well."

"Did you bring your beverages?" Bev asked. "There's cups and ice over at that corner table if you need it."

I held up my bottles of beer. "That's great. Victoria, can I take your wine over and pour you a glass?"

She handed me the bottle and said to the others, "Guilt is a wonderful thing. I'm going to let her wait on me hand and foot as long as it lasts."

Teri and I went to the bar table. After taking care of our drinks, we put the rest of the wine and my extra beer in a large galvanized tub of ice.

"Grab a koozie," Glynis said. "Everyone gets one." She pointed to a pile of bandana printed koozies. I picked one up and thought maybe it was a good item with which to experiment taking something back with me.

Glynis whistled for attention and asked everyone to find a place at a table. Once that was done, she picked the table in the middle to begin the buffet line.

Roasters of barbecued pulled pork and chicken gave off wonderful aromas. I also selected a creamy coleslaw and a fruit salad.

Back at our table, Melanie proposed a toast. Conversation centered on upcoming Sisters events. Since I wouldn't be around (and wasn't a member), my mind and eyes wandered to the other tables. Although most of the attire had a western theme, there was the odd tiger costume and Raggedy Ann wig.

As we finished our meal, Glynis and two others dressed as dance hall girls, came around with dessert trays. Small individual galvanized buckets contained layers of chocolate cake, ice cream, nuts, and chocolate sauce. Each had a small black cowgirl silhouette stuck in the top. Noises of appreciation were soon quieted as everyone dug in.

While the band came in and set up, we cleared the dishes and got the food put away in coolers under Glynis' direction.

It didn't take long for the women to warm up to the music, with a little help from the beer and wine, and they were out dancing in ones, twos, and threes. When the trio played a line dance, they all cheered and performed like a professional dance team. Well, almost.

A crack of thunder and a celestial flash of lightning barely caused a pause; only a few glanced at the windows. But I watched. I sat most of the time with Victoria, who I could tell was not up for that much frolicking. The rain started pounding the clear plastic weather shades that had been lowered in anticipation of the storm.

About 9:00, the power failed. The lanterns, of course, stayed lit, but the amplifiers and electric instruments died with kind of a disappointed groan. Everyone waited around for a few minutes to see if it would come back on, but no such luck. The lanterns on the tables cast enough light for minimal functioning. One of the rangers pulled up in a pickup and ran to the door covering his head.

Inside, he pushed the door shut and pulled off his cap. I half expected him to shake like a dog.

"I just came to check on y'all. Power company said the power may be off all night." He looked at the band. They looked at Glynis.

She shrugged and said, "That's probably long enough

for us old ladies anyway. Let's give 'em a hand girls!" She led the applause. The band members bowed and thanked the group while they started packing up.

I walked over to Glynis and the ranger.

"What's the forecast?" I asked him.

"More of this." He glanced outside.

"Is there a chance of flash flooding? I mean, some of those sites are awfully close to the river."

First he shook his head. "We haven't gotten any warnings." Then he looked outside again. "But you know, with it coming down like this, it might not be a bad idea to move your people in the tents up to higher ground. Could you do that?"

Glynis looked alarmed. "That's no problem—what about our trailers that are by the tents? Should we move those too?"

"Like I said, we haven't actually gotten a warning so it's up to you. Might be wise."

Glynis stuck two fingers in her mouth and produced a piercing whistle. The ranger covered his ears.

"Ladies!" Glynis yelled and clapped her hands. They all turned toward her and she explained the situation. "This is precautionary, but I think we need to get your tents and Victoria's and my trailers up off the bank if we can. We're going to need everyone's help." She turned to the ranger. "Can we park them anywhere for tonight?"

"Don't block the road in case we need to get emergency vehicles in. Can you move them as far as the parking lot at the shower house?"

"Once we get them hooked up, we can move them anywhere. Thanks!"

Sisters were already pulling down laundry, picking up bandanas and throwing them in the plastic tubs that we had stored under the bar table. A few of the women who had been forward thinking enough to bring raincoats barged out with the tubs to put them in Glynis' truck. The lanterns were kept lit until we were finished and Glynis, Teri, and I extinguished them and carried them out. The rain was relentless and it was difficult to even see our way to the vehicles without the security lights.

Back at the campsites, we braced ourselves to face the rain and piled back out of the vehicles. Several were already pulling down tents and throwing items in cars and trucks. Teri went to hook up Victoria's camper while I helped Glynis with her flags and other paraphernalia. She had already put away many things and I wanted to tell her to leave everything else and get out of there but knew I couldn't.

It was getting hard to see with the rain running down my face. We managed to get Glynis' trailer hooked up and I rode with her to park it at the shower house. We hurried through the unhooking process and climbed back in her truck. I tried to wipe the water off my face with my hand without much luck.

Teri arrived pulling Victoria's trailer, so back out in the driving rain we went to help and told Victoria to stay in the truck. When we returned to our campsites, the others were inside various trailers, having done what they could to clear the bank. Victoria was going to stay with Teri and Glynis would stay with me, but for the time being, we all went in Teri's trailer. Teri handed out towels and while we dried ourselves as well as we could, she rummaged in a cupboard and produced a bottle of whiskey.

"Something to warm the innards?" she asked. In the back of another cabinet she found four shot glasses.

Everyone accepted. I've never been a big whiskey drinker but at the moment, it sounded perfect.

"There's one trailer still down on the bank," Victoria said. "Someone not in our group."

"Maybe the owners aren't there," Glynis said. "The Ranger was going to tell everyone."

Teri sat down and leaned back against the cushions on the sofa. "I guess it's better to be safe than sorry but I've never heard of this river coming up that much."

Glynis frowned. "I haven't either but I suppose it's possible. All of those rock walls probably act like a funnel."

We sat quietly for a minute, sipping our whiskey and listening to the rain and wind batter the sides of the camper. So far, I felt pretty good about the way things were going. I had been agonizing over excuses to get people away from the river's edge—snake sightings, for example. Who knew that a simple suggestion of possible flash flooding to the ranger would get everyone moved out of harm's way?

"Will the ranger or someone come around if they get any kind of warning of bad weather?" I asked.

Teri laughed. "What do you think this is?" She indicated the noise going on outside.

We all laughed then, releasing a little tension. Soon I could tell Victoria was drooping. She was right—I would carry the guilt for her injury forever. However, I wouldn't be able to wait on her after tomorrow.

"I think we should let Victoria get some rest," I said to Glynis.

"Absolutely," Glynis said. "Could you bring your Jeep right up to the steps? So I don't have to get wet?"

"I could but we might be there all night."

Teri pulled out a couple of garbage bags and handed them to us. "Here. Don't get yourselves any wetter."

"Thanks," I said. We used a scissors to cut out holes for our faces and hands. When we put them on, Teri and Victoria broke up.

"You look like some cartoon characters from a really dumb commercial," Victoria said.

"Hey," Glynis said. "We don't make fun of the hole in your head."

We hurried out the door and picked our way down the steps, with me going first. I put my foot down on the ground and it slid down the muddy slope, my other foot catching on the bottom step. It came loose with a twist as

I slid face down toward the road. I came to a rest a few feet down the hill and pain shot through my ankle and leg.

"Lynne!" Glynis bent over me, the rain streaming off her garbage bag and getting me even wetter.

I groaned and pushed myself up. "I'm okay. Help me up and we'll get to the Jeep."

"What happened?" Teri called from the door. "Do you need help?" Her words were almost lost in a crash of thunder.

"No!" I yelled back. "Stay inside! See you in the morning."

Glynis got me up and together we hobbled and slipped toward my Jeep. Flashes of lightning gave a little visibility but it was a lot like trying to follow dance step patterns under a strobe light. Although I can't say I've ever done that.

"You want me to drive?" Glynis yelled in my ear when we got to the car.

I shook my head. "It's my left ankle. I'll be okay."

She helped me into the driver's seat and then rushed around to the passenger side. Once we were both inside, we leaned back and looked at each other, wet faces peering out of our garbage bags.

I burst out laughing. "This is stupid."

"I agree," she said. "We should go get a motel."

It was tempting but I knew I needed to stay at the campground so I shook my head. "It'll be okay when we get inside my trailer." I started the Jeep, put the wipers on at high speed, and we edged our way up the campground road to the next level where my trailer was parked. I handed Glynis the keys and she got the trailer unlocked while I hobbled up to the door.

Glynis pulled her garbage bag off and tried to wring it out in the sink.

"Those didn't help much," she said.

I struggled out of mine. "I don't think anything would in this kind of storm." I got a plastic grocery sack out of the cupboard. "Can we put them in here?"

We proceeded to set the beds up with me mostly giving direction. I loaned her a sweat suit—checking first that the shirt didn't say something like 'Soccer Mom 2012'—while I pulled on some flannel pajamas.

We piled all of our wet clothes in another sack. "We'll have to find a laundromat tomorrow," she said. "I'm ready to crash. How about you?"

"Absolutely." I had a feeling it would be a short night as far as sleep was concerned and made sure my shoes were where I could get them. I don't think blankets and a bed had ever felt so good in my life, but it didn't bring me much peace.

CHAPTER 19

I THOUGHT I would be able to stay awake but I must have dozed because the banging on the door startled me.

"Hello?" I heard a woman call over the still-pounding rain. Glynis was already up and at the door. She had the foresight to grab a flashlight — or may have been sleeping with it for all I knew. Through the open door, I could see the woman ranger who had done the snake search of Bev's tent.

"We got a flash flood warning," she said. "Now we want everyone to move to higher ground. We're opening the nature center farther up the hill."

My first reaction was resignation, and then, a few moments later, out and out panic. What if my trailer got washed away? I would never get back to my own time! Although I had talked to Ben about going back in my own lifetime, I still wasn't clear whether there was another me relaxing on my back porch, perhaps coloring with a five-year-old Dinah or how this worked. Then I calmed down a bit. I had read the accounts of the flood. Only the sites along the bank were affected. My trailer would be okay, and so would I if I stayed with it.

Glynis had closed the door and grabbed her clothes off the end of the bed.

"You go. I'm staying here," I said. "I can't explain but I know I'll be fine."

"What? You can't know that! You have a daughter to think of."

That was exactly my reason for staying. I couldn't take a chance on anything happening to my trailer. I would go ahead and hook it up and if it did look like the water was coming up this high, I would leave and head back to the campground where I had changed times.

She pulled her clothes on, but I could see by her face she was conflicted. "I have to go. My daughter has already lost her father and I have to be there for her kids —not just to babysit but to help maintain continuity." Tears were starting to run down her face.

I went to her and hugged her. "I'll be fine," I repeated. "Absolutely, you should go. I'm going to hook up my trailer and probably pull it out of here. Do you want me to give you a ride up the hill first?"

She straightened and wiped her eyes. "No, I'll go

down and get my truck and some things I don't want to lose from my trailer. I don't even have my purse or ID or bank cards or anything." She fished around in the sack for one of the garbage bags and put it on. It was still wet. I held the door for her as she picked her way down the steps and the muddy slope.

"Don't fall!" I called after her. I should talk. She waved a hand and kept going. Before I closed the door, I scanned the campground. Vehicle headlights were coming on at various sites and dark shapes rushed around carrying bundles.

I got dressed, and found a rain slicker I had stashed in one of the cupboards. At least it would be better than a garbage bag. My ankle was still sore; I needed to be very careful not to twist it again.

I packed the camper for travel as quickly as I could and went outside to hook it up. The area at the hitch end was a muddy mire. By the time I got ready to back the Jeep up, most of the others had gone. I put it in four-wheel drive and started to back up.

The muddy slope, the driving rain, and the darkness all combined to make it one of the biggest challenges of my life. In spite of the four-wheel drive, the direction was not straight and true by any means. I got out several times to check my progress, if you could call it that.

The campground seemed deserted but there lights left on in a few campers — whether forgotten or left on to welcome the owners back when this was over was hard to say.

I finally got the trailer hooked up after losing a pin in the mud and nearly falling twice. I sat in the jeep, dried my face with an old rag, and debated my options. I should get out now. But I had a niggling feeling that I would be abandoning ship after coming all this way without knowing if I had accomplished my mission. I assumed that Bev and Melanie had joined the others up at the Nature Center but felt I needed to be sure.

I held my breath and would have crossed my fingers if I hadn't needed them to drive. Slowly I pulled out of the campsite onto the campground road. Leaning over the wheel, I peered between the wipers. All I could see was about three feet of road and the rain in the headlights.

As I crept around a curve, I gasped at the reflection of the headlights on water. The river was already up to the first road. I couldn't go through that way. I got out of the Jeep, cringing at facing the slashing rain again and trudged back the way I came.

There was another road about fifty feet back and I thought I could possibly back up that far. Before I did though, I wanted to check Melanie's trailer to see if she and Bev had heeded the warnings. Her site was right above this road so I climbed a small hill and edged around the back of Sandy's little Shasta.

There was a light on in Melanie's trailer. I climbed the steps and pounded on the door. No response. I tried the door and it opened.

"Melanie?" I called. "Bev?" Still no response. That was good; they must have gone to higher ground. I could now leave, at least the area, satisfied that I had done what I could.

I hobbled back to the Jeep. I had left it running and the lights on; the water had almost reached the front tires. No time to waste. I opened the door to climb in but stopped.

A shout was coming from nearer the river. A man's voice I thought, although over the wind, rain, and roar of the river, it was hard to be sure. I pulled a large flashlight from under the seat and slammed the door.

I walked along the edge of the road toward the sound. It was getting closer and sounded like a cry for help. As I swept the beam of light across the water, I was shocked at the debris—tents, branches, and even a car hurtling along in the current.

There was a truck, too—not far from the water's edge that wasn't moving. I trained the flashlight back on it. A man stood on the hood waving his arms and yelling. Behind him was the trailer we had noticed earlier that hadn't been moved.

It was Gary, the jerk from the bar. I resisted an impulse to tell him there were no men around who could help him. The water was swirling around the truck and would no doubt soon carry it downstream.

I looked around and couldn't see anything useful at

first, but then spotted a loop of rope left from a tent or something, laying in a campsite. Teri's kayak lay beside her trailer.

I got the rope, tied it on the bow of the kayak and dragged it to the water's edge, the whole time seething. If I lost my camper because of this jerk, I would drown him myself.

I pulled the kayak upstream of the truck to a point where I could tie the other end of the rope to a tree and let the current take the boat down to him. I let the rope out slowly, fighting the current and kept the flashlight on the boat so he could see what was coming. When he figured it out, he laid down on the truck hood, arms out stretched in preparation.

At first the boat wanted to drift past the truck so I had to keep pulling it back to try again. Finally, the kayak bumped up against the side of the truck and he managed to reach it. He tried to step in from the hood with no success so slipped off the hood into the water.

He floundered, trying to keep his balance in the raging water. It couldn't have been very deep there but the current made standing upright impossible. He tipped the kayak over several times but couldn't get in.

"Hang on!" I yelled. I don't know if he heard me or just gave up trying to climb in from exhaustion. Anyway, he clung to the stern and looked back at me helplessly.

I started to pull the rope back. My arms ached, my sore ankle throbbed and I wanted desperately to turn around and see what was happening to my trailer.

It seemed like it took forever to get him about twenty feet to where he was able to get some footing and push himself along, relieving some of the strain on my arms. I finally was able to drag the kayak above the water line and reach for him. He lay on the ground gasping and trying to talk.

"I can't swim...The camper — I couldn't pull it out — it was too late — "

What? Did he think I was going to rescue his camper, too?

"She got pulled away — "

Realization dawned.

"Your wife? Where is she?"

"She — she — " he pointed wildly. "The water — " he turned to his side and coughed. He lay back down. "She couldn' make it t' the truck."

"The river washed her away?" I wanted to shake him. He nodded. I grabbed my flashlight and got up.

"Wait," he said. "Thanks — "

"Oh shut up." I ran as best I could along the edge of the water, past where Gary's truck was now being pulled into the current. I didn't know his wife's name so I called out, "Hello? Are you there?"

I stumbled and caught myself before I went down, stood up and used the flashlight to sweep the area. It seemed like the rain was a little lighter but it may have been my imagination.

As the beam of light crossed a clump of trees, I caught a glimpse of light blue in one of the trees and tried to hold the light on it. An arm waved. I didn't know if it was Gary's wife or someone else who had been caught but it didn't matter. I went back for the kayak and found the paddle where I had thrown it on the ground.

This was insane, I knew. My paddling skills were next to nonexistent in this kind of situation. I had my phone in the Jeep but had gotten 'no service' messages the whole weekend.

I really had no choice.

Gary was getting to his feet, so as I pulled the kayak along the wet grass, I yelled to him, "Get some help!"

"I don't know what happened to my phone," he whined.

"I don't care how you do it! I said, get some help. Get up and get moving!" I was steaming. Having to be rescued by a woman had knocked him down a few pegs but leaving his wife out there and not telling me until he was safe really tripped my trigger.

The kayak was still tied to the tree and my fingers fumbled with the knot of wet rope to no avail. I couldn't get it loose. I returned to my Jeep and fumbled around in the console for a utility knife. The water was still rising around the wheels. Back at the tree, I slashed through the rope, pretending it was Gary's neck.

I started to stomp back down the road pulling the boat but when pain shot through my ankle, thought better of it. When I got just upriver again from the clump of trees, I used my light to scan the trees. The light blue jacket or shirt was still there.

The water had come across the first road but hadn't progressed farther since I got Gary out. I tied one end of the rope around a registration post at the edge of the road. With the kayak at the very edge of the water, I stepped in, sat down, and managed to push off with the paddle. The current quickly took control and pulled me out away from the edge. I paddled furiously, aiming for where I thought the trees were.

Suddenly, I spun around and became totally disoriented. I hoped the rope held and would right my direction. I grabbed the light from the bottom of the kayak to check where I was. Looming in front of me and bobbing in the water like a toy was Gary's camper.

I tried back-paddling but only succeeded in going in circles. I held the paddle in front of me to avoid a straight-on crash with the camper. As I rocked up and down and banged against the aluminum sides, I tried to work my way around the obstacle.

I stowed my paddle and reached over the stern to the rope, using it to pull me back around the camper. I managed to release the rope from the snags as I went and received several cuts on my hands for my efforts. Once free of the camper, I continued to strain toward the edge of the water. Until the camper floated out of the way, I couldn't reach the trees.

I was exhausted. I could feel the tears of frustration streaming down my face as I inched my way back. My hands felt raw from gripping the rope. The muscles in my arms burned. The dark water swirled around me, and although it couldn't be terribly deep, I knew the current and the debris could be my end.

But I couldn't go any farther. I collapsed draped over the stern of the boat, my hands locked around the rope. Lightning continued to flash and I hoped it didn't signal more rain. The faces of my family floated in my head— Kurt, Dinah, my mother. I was too tired to cry any more and zoned out.

Then I realized that the lightning had a strange tinted quality to it. At the same time, I became aware of voices in the distance. I raised my head and looked toward shore. Several emergency vehicles sat at crazy angles, lights flashing red and blue. Dark shadows scurried around in the headlights.

"Help!" I called, very feebly. One figure was shouting something to me through cupped hands. I noticed an inflatable boat heading toward me, propelled by an engine. I couldn't even feel relief, I was so tired.

Strong arms pulled me into the boat and I had a moment of worry about the kayak but remembered it was tethered to the post. As if that was the most crucial issue at the time.

We quickly returned to the water's edge and I regained my voice enough to tell them about Gary's wife.

"We're looking for her," said a deep-voiced, rain-slickered man. "Can you show us where you think you saw her?"

He was helping me out of the boat and I pointed down river. He helped me walk along the water, followed by two other rescuers, one pulling the boat and the other carrying a stretcher. When we were even with the clump of trees, I directed one of them to shine their industrial-strength flashlight in that direction. The light blue shirt or whatever was in the water, caught among the trees.

"That's her—at least I assume it is. I was trying to get to her but couldn't get around the camper—"

They were already in the inflatable, pushing off far enough to get the motor started. Another person shrouded in yellow took my arm.

"Ma'am?" he said. "We need to get you warm."

"But, I want to see—"

He shook his head. "You'll have hypothermia unless we get you treated."

He guided me back up to the emergency vehicles. Gary sat in the back of a rescue vehicle, wrapped in a blanket and looking very sorry for himself. The water was about six inches up on the wheels of my Jeep.

"Please," I said to my rescuer, "I need to get my car and camper out of the water and in a safe place."

Gary scoffed. "I lost a camper worth a lot more than that piece of junk of yours."

Apparently, I was no longer his hero.

"Your ignorance is showing," I replied. The first responder, who had been pulling out a blanket for me, looked from one to the other of us, perplexed.

I moved away from Gary and motioned the tech to follow. He put the blanket around my shoulders.

"You need to sit down, ma'am, so I can check your vitals," he said, in a tone meant to convince small children and the insane.

"I hate to be difficult, but I *have* to get that trailer backed up to where it will stay safe. I can't explain *why* it is so important, but it *is*. I refuse any treatment until that is done." I took the blanket off to hand it back to him.

"Do you want to drive or should I?"

"Oh, for God's sake!" I heard Gary say in the background. Still a jerk.

"I'll drive, " I said, and got in the Jeep, squishing as I sat down. I lowered the window and pointed to where I wanted to go. "If you'll just direct me so I can get this out of the water, then I will do whatever you say."

He moved back and used his flashlight to get me turned the way I wanted. I finally had the whole rig up on the second road, facing the exit.

When I got out and thanked the young man, he said, "I think the water has stopped rising."

"Well, I hope so but I have to be sure. Thank you again." We returned to the emergency vehicles.

I sat meekly while he replaced the blanket and took my temperature and pulse. The rain had stopped and the thunder rumbled quietly in the distance.

"What about my wife?" Gary demanded of the tech.

"They're working on it sir." He looked down the road. "Here they come." Two of the guys quick-stepped along carrying a stretcher while the other pulled the inflatable boat back against the current.

One of the techs motioned for Gary to move out of the ambulance so they could slide the stretcher in. A little concern showed on his face.

"Is she — ?"

"She's unconscious but still breathing. Do you want to ride along?"

"Um. . . sure."

Like he had to think about it?

A tech helped him get in beside his wife while another got in the driver's seat, started the vehicle up and turned on the siren. Soon they were on their way out of the campground.

CHAPTER

20

WHILE OTHERS LOADED the boat in the rescue unit, the guy who had helped me said, "Don't you think you should be checked out? We have another ambulance here."

I shook my head. I didn't want any more questions about identity or anyone looking for my records.

"I'll be fine." I looked at my watch. Almost 5:00 a.m. "I'm going to say goodbye to the people at the Nature Center and then get on the road." I glanced up at the sky. Wisps of pink light appeared in the east. "Is there any more rain forecast?"

"No. How far do you have to go?"

"About seven hours." Of course I wasn't going to do all of it in one day. I first had to hang out until night at the park where I had time traveled back ten years and hope that the process reversed itself. I was ready to get out of this place before I screwed up any more time lines.

The Nature Center was on the main road out of the park. I left the campground, turned left away from the river, and climbed the moderate grade of the main road.

About halfway up the hill, a rustic log building sat at the back of a parking lot. A lot full of cars and pickups and lights on all over the building were not typical, I was sure, for this hour of the morning. I chose a spot at the edge of the lot where I would not have to do any backing and just pulled my rig along the curb.

As I exited the Jeep, I caught sight of myself in the side mirror. A drowned rat would not be flattered to be compared to me. My clothes were still damp and my hair hung in dirty clumps around my face. A streak of mud swept from my chin to my ear.

I went back to the trailer, grabbed clean clothes, a towel, washcloth, soap, and shampoo and stuffed them in a bag. I didn't expect the Nature Center to have a shower but hot water and a sink would do.

I pushed open the front door and saw the refugees from the night in clusters around a large room, some curled up on the floor and some sitting and talking quietly in small groups. I spotted Glynis, Teri, and Victoria sitting against a wooden stand holding a tank of turtles. They waved me over.

"What happened?" Teri said, her eyes taking in my less than spiffy appearance.

I explained the predicament of Gary and his wife and their subsequent rescue.

"Oh, my God!" Glynis said. "You poor thing! Are they okay?"

"I think so. At least Gary is, although it doesn't seem to have improved his personality. His wife was breathing when they put her in the ambulance. She couldn't have been in the water too long, because she had waved at me before I tried to rescue her."

I paused, trying to remember the sequence of events. "I guess I really don't know how long that took…" I pushed my hair back. "I'm going to try and clean up a little bit. I assume there's a restroom here?"

Victoria pointed to a short hallway. "Do you need any help?"

I grimaced. "I need a *lot* of help but unless you're a beautician or plastic surgeon, I think I'll just make do."

They all laughed and waved me off. I found the restroom and washed my hair as best I could in the shallow sink. At least the clumps of mud and weeds were gone.

Then I stripped down, gave myself a sponge bath, and put on clean clothes. I was a new woman, except for the sore ankle, cuts on my hands, and other aches and pains. I looked at the soggy pile of clothes on the floor, scooped them up, and dumped them in the trash.

When I returned to the main room, a couple of the Sisters and Lil, the campground hostess, were helping the woman ranger lay out breakfast from a large box of styrofoam containers on a table that probably only been used to dissect snakes or something in the past. Nobody cared. Melanie and Bev waved me over and made me get ahead of them in line.

"How are you?" Melanie said, her voice filled with concern.

"Much better now that I'm sort of clean."

"What an experience! We're *all* lucky that you were here. You were the one who warned about a possible flash flood." Melanie gave me a hug while Bev patted me on the back.

We dished up paper plates of scrambled eggs, sausages, and even pancakes. The ranger said one of the local restaurants had donated the food. Someone had found a closet of folding chairs and set several up so we didn't have to sit on the floor. The food tasted wonderful and completed my restoration.

I told the women while we were eating that I was going to take off as soon as we were done.

"It's a long trip, and I think I'm ready to see my family and sleep in my own bed."

Teri put her plate down on the floor and dug in a pocket, producing a little notebook with a pen. "Give me your cell number. Let's keep in touch, and I'll let you know about future Sister events, if you decide to join."

I laughed. "I'm not sure I can take any more of these 'relaxing' weekends." I debated about the phone number but decided it couldn't hurt. It was a fairly new one and if she tried it, she would either get someone else or a disconnect message and that would be that. So I dictated the number and she wrote it down.

After breakfast there were hugs all around and wishes for a safe journey. I told them they were an amazing group and I meant it. I was glad I came.

THE STORM HAD PASSED and the sky couldn't have been any bluer. The winds were light so I didn't have any trouble staying on the road. Again the rolling hills and vivid greens brought peace to my mind. For all of the troubles, everything had turned out okay.

I stopped for gas and rechecked the route to the state park near Lurleen. It wasn't far and within the hour I was pulling up to the guard shack. The same older man I had waved goodbye to on Thursday was on duty. If he remembered me, he didn't show it. I pulled to the side again and walked up to the window.

"Good morning!" I said when he slid open the sash. "I'm looking for a campsite for tonight. I was wondering if site #26 is available."

"Well, let me check." He looked at the map fastened to a clipboard. As he did so, he wrinkled his forehead and scratched the top of his head though wispy white hair. "It isn't right now but they're supposed to be checking out today. We have several other sites available — real nice ones."

"I really like that site. Maybe I'll go into town for some lunch and come back later. When's check out time?"

"Two o'clock, ma'am." I could tell he thought I was being pretty picky. He probably chalked it up to finicky womanhood.

I thanked him and returned to my car. I managed to get the trailer turned without taking out any trees by circling the guard shack. I turned toward Lurleen and drove along the main street looking for a restaurant.

It wasn't nearly time for lunch but I didn't know where else I could hang out for a few hours. I spotted a convenience store first and pulled in to buy a daily paper. I wondered if the flood and near disaster would have been covered yet. As I paid for the paper, I asked about a restaurant. The young clerk looked at me like I had landed from space.

"We don't have anyplace open on *Sunday*."

Okay then. Good thing I had my own little house with me.

"I need to pick up some other things then. Would it be okay if I pulled my trailer over to the side of your lot for a few hours? I'm waiting for a spot to open up at the state park."

She tipped her head and stared at me. "You mean park it there? On our lot?"

"You know what? Forget it." I went back through the store and picked up a large cup of coffee, a couple of cream-filled donuts that were probably fresh the day before, a box of crackers, a block of cheddar, and for good measure, a banana. The clerk was too busy watching a young man gas up his car out the front window to carry on a conversation while she rang me up, so I took my purchases and left.

I had noticed a large trucking concern on the edge of town with a huge gravel lot and figured I wouldn't bother anyone there on a Sunday. If so, I could move. So I pulled in there, parked at the back edge, and took my paper and my treats back to the trailer.

The newspaper had a small story at the bottom of the front page. Basically, it said there had been a flash flood at Paulie's Shoots, that several campers needed to be rescued, and the rest had moved to higher ground.

Although one woman was in the hospital in serious condition, there were no reported fatalities. Very good. I drank my coffee and ate one of the donuts while I read my book for a while and realized what I really needed was sleep. It had been a short night. I was still wearing the 2005 Christmas charm on a chain around my neck and wasn't worried about being transported in time. And if I was, was that so bad? It was what I hoped for anyway.

I was soon fast asleep.

I WOKE IN a sweat—the camper had heated up in the warm sun—and looked at my watch. It was 3:00 in the afternoon. I sat up, stretched, ate another donut, and drove back to the park. Once I was back in site #26, I had a lot of time to kill. I decided the first order of business was a real shower.

That taken care of, I made a light supper of the crackers, cheese, and the banana. After all of the great food that weekend, the big breakfast and two cream donuts, I needed to make amends. I went for a walk around the campground.

It seems so often that after Mother Nature has released her fury, she tries to compensate with a golden soft evening, and it works. A few lazy bugs swam in the fading sunlight and most of the campsites were empty. The weekend was over and the campground was at rest. I returned to my trailer, took off the 2005 charm and went to bed.

CHAPTER
21

THE NEXT MORNING, I experienced a familiar ambivalence when I woke up. I lay in bed wondering if I had returned to 2015, but reluctant to get up and find out for sure. It was never obvious and involved finding a newspaper or TV because people looked at you funny if you asked them what year it was.

In an inspired moment, I reached toward the floor and pulled my purse toward me. When I found my phone, I turned it on. The screen lit up and little chimes played. The month and day were there, but not the year. I must be back if I had reception.

The campground was as quiet and lovely as it had been the night before (ten years earlier.) The dew on the grass sparkled in the morning sun and a few butterflies hovered in the wildflowers that bordered the site. I removed the 2002 license plates.

I still felt disoriented or something. I had managed to change the timeline so that two lives were saved, but now I wondered how that affected things going forward. Would Melanie/Naomi still have landed at the day care in my small town? I didn't think so.

And if not, would Kurt and Dinah know where I was and why? I usually tried not to think about the conundrum of time travel much because it just made my head hurt. Once again, I waved at the attendant in the guard shack as I pulled out of the campground. This time it was the concerned woman who on Thursday was worried that I was being abused.

As I cruised along the highway, appreciating the good weather and light traffic, I wished I could turn on the radio to catch up on the weekend news. It occurred to me that there could have been a major tragedy or even a personal one. What if Kurt and Dinah had been in an accident and I wasn't there for them?

My phone, laying on the passenger seat, rang. I picked it up and glanced at the screen. It was Kurt. I was going to stop for gas and coffee anyway in the next few miles, so decided I would call him back then.

I found a small old convenience store. Not fancy but it had the requisite gas and coffee. Kurt answered on the first ring.

"Lynne! Where are you?"

"Missouri. I'm on my way home."

"What are you doing down there? I drove out to Ben's and I see the trailer is gone."

He was angry but trying to control it. I sighed. As I suspected, the time line had changed enough that my trip now made no sense to him, if it ever did.

"It's a long story. I'll be home in about three hours. Can I meet you for a late lunch?"

"Lynne, I wish you'd get rid of that thing—it's been nothing but trouble. Anyway, how about the Frog?"

"That would be great. One o'clock?"

"See you then." He hung up.

Well. I felt like my brain was in a blender and all my thoughts and concerns were smushed together so that none were distinguishable. I couldn't really come up with an argument for keeping the trailer. Although I was pleased with the overall results of the weekend, there were too many close calls and I was learning that the timeline probably shouldn't be messed with.

The rest of the trip I tried to think about other things. I should be planning some sort of trip—sans camper—with Dinah before the summer got away. After all, I'm a travel agent; I could come up with something. Maybe Kurt would want to join us—we had been making progress in getting back together.

I considered a cruise, but then thought about a dude ranch. Dinah loves horseback riding and there were lots of places that catered to families so there would be other young people. Before I knew it, I was at my exit. I managed to get the trailer parked and some things unloaded by noon so I had time for a shower before I had to meet Kurt.

As I WALKED into the Frog an hour later, I felt pretty good. I still felt a glow of satisfaction from the weekend and my own shower helped. Kurt was sitting in a booth on the side. He looked up as I approached but he didn't smile. Oh-oh.

"Hi," I said. I leaned over to kiss him on the cheek and he backed away.

"You're angry," I said, as I sat down.

Sandra brought us water and took out her order pad. "What can I get you today?"

I ordered salad and Kurt perused the menu, finally selecting a hot beef sandwich. He wouldn't look at me.

"Kurt," I began, after Sandra left, "I can explain but you may not believe it."

He sighed--his favorite response. With an effort, he said, "Let's hear it."

"Do you know Naomi Burks?"

He shook his head. "Never heard of her."

This was going to get sticky. I explained how I had met her, her suicide attempt, and my decision to go back in time and try and save her friend. The more I talked, the more skeptical he looked.

"You're saying that you told me about this before?"

181

"Yes, but when I went back and suggested that the ranger move people away from the bank in case of a flood, Bev's life was saved, and apparently Naomi—or Melanie, as her real name is—didn't go into depression and never moved here. So the timeline has changed."

He kept shaking his head. "This kind of thing never happened last year when we—", he looked around the restaurant and lowered his voice, "you know, went back."

"We didn't change anything. Or at least not enough to affect the present day as we know it."

He took a different approach. "You know how frightened we were last summer when Dinah disappeared. Imagine how *she* felt when you were gone and so was the trailer. We're adults—she's *fifteen*. We had no idea where you were."

I hung my head a little. "I didn't think about what could happen to the timeline as far as our lives are concerned until I was on my way home."

"No, you didn't think."

Sandra brought our food and we thanked her. We didn't say any more for a few minutes as we started on our food.

Kurt put down his fork. "I'm thinking about requesting full custody of Dinah."

"What?" I almost choked on a piece of tomato.

"This is too serious. You've gone over the edge about this trailer thing and you don't consider how it will affect us."

"You can't do that. I'm her mother and a responsible parent."

"You used to be," he said. "I have an appointment with Brad Burns to talk about it." Brad was Kurt's lawyer.

I pushed my salad away. I had lost my appetite, but I had a thought. "How are you going to show a court that I'm a bad mother? Are you going to tell them that I time travel?"

"No, of course not. But I could tell them that you disappeared without telling us and Dinah was very scared."

"She was only scared because she knows what the trailer can do. No court is going to believe that. Besides it was your weekend to have her. My leaving for four days doesn't constitute abandonment. You've left town when she's with me and not told us."

I paused to catch my breath. I was clutching air trying to regain my balance. I had walked in here feeling pretty good. After all of the stress leading to the weekend, it had worked out well. And in the last year, Kurt and I had taken steps to rebuild our marriage. Was this the trade off —that I would lose my family to save two lives?

I fished in my purse and threw a ten on the table. "I have to think," I said. "I'll call you tonight." And I left.

THE AFTERNOON WAS miserable. Dinah was working at the pool all day. I sat on my porch and alternated between tears and anger. How could Kurt do this? But then, when I put myself in his place, I could see his concern and Dinah's fear.

They were sure I had time traveled but had no way of knowing, in this timeline, how far back I had gone or if I would ever return. There was no way to have avoided it. I could wait a year for the proper date and go back again and reverse things. Not give Dinah such a fright and get my reconciliation back on track with Kurt. And sacrifice two lives. No, of course I *couldn't* do that.

I had to do something. One decision I made absolutely: I would not be using the trailer again.

I got a couple of totes and went out to unload every item I had put in it. Once that was done, I closed and locked it. Maybe Ben could help me decide how to deal with it. It seemed to me that burning it would be the best solution. I put the key on a chain around my neck.

By the time I was back inside, fixing a simple supper, I heard the back door slam and my daughter's voice.

"Mom?" She stomped up the half flight of steps, hands on hips. "Dad said you were home. Where have you been?"

I opened my arms and she fell into them sobbing. I let her cry a little and then led her out to the porch.

"Why didn't you tell us what you were doing?" she said, wiping her nose. "When Dad said the trailer was gone, I couldn't believe you didn't leave a note."

We sat down at the table. "Honey," I said, "actually

you were the one who first suggested this trip. You and Daddy knew all about it. However, what I did while I was gone changed the timeline and wiped that all out. I never considered that that might happen." I explained about Naomi Burks, her depression and her suicide attempt. I told her about the Sisters on the Fly event at Paulie's Shoots and the flash flooding.

"So you see, the two women who died in the original timeline survived. As a result, Melanie never changed her name or came to our town to start over. Therefore, neither you nor Dad knew anything about her or this event."

She sat with her mouth open, thinking. I could see the wheels turning.

"Very hard to grasp, isn't it? I'm still struggling with it."

"Nothing like that happened when we 'traveled' last year," she said.

"We don't really know. We didn't cause any changes that affected us directly. But we may have caused changes that we don't know about. This is the end for that camper. I'll talk to Ben about it. As far as I'm concerned, I think it should be burned."

Now she was shocked. "Really? You would do that?"

"Definitely. There's too many 'what ifs' and 'if this, then that'. We can't begin to know what effects our actions have. I don't know if your dad will ever forgive me — or trust me again." I started to tear up.

She leaned over and hugged me."He will. I know he will."

It was her fifteen-year-old optimism speaking. Our roles had reversed, with her first scolding and then reassuring me.

THE NEXT TWO weeks dragged by slowly, even though I was very busy. I didn't have time to talk to Ben; the camper sat behind our garage holding its secrets. Kurt called the second week to make arrangements to pick up Dinah for the weekend. Custody was not mentioned; neither was forgiveness or understanding. I was afraid to bring any of it up.

Late one night, I finished up some research on Ireland for a client and thought back to my weekend with the Sisters on the Fly. I looked up their website.

I had been so impressed with the supportiveness of the group that after looking over the site, I signed up for a membership. It said I would be notified within forty-eight hours of my acceptance. I looked over some of the sample events — from fly fishing and horseback riding to wine tasting and crafts. I went to bed.

The next day, I had forgotten my application in a rush of clients and an orthodontist appointment for Dinah.

The switch in the timeline caused issues at work as well. I had several clients that I didn't have in the timeline of my memory; I had to scramble and bluff my through those appointments, pretending I knew what they were talking about. There were others who were gone from my files, including of course, Melanie.

When I got home from work, I sat down to check personal email while a roast finished cooking. My acceptance and Sister number were in the inbox. I went back to the website but was disappointed that there wasn't a member list.

There was, however, a list of trailer names, identified by the Sister numbers, and I was pleased that Glynis' *Luella* and Victoria's *Her Majesty* were there. I couldn't remember the name of Teri's or if she even had one. I didn't know about Melanie either.

While I was thinking about it, I googled Melanie. She had an up to date profile on LinkedIn and a Facebook page. Things must have worked out for her then.

I went back to the Sisters' website and looked over coming events in the Midwest. There was a Junk Jaunt at a park about sixty miles from me coming up in about a month and a fly fishing event in Michigan in the fall.

I wasn't sure if I wanted to try another camper or not. Maybe one of the new retro reproductions, but definitely nothing old.

I ran into Ben and Minnie at church the next Sunday. We sat together afterward at coffee hour, and I wanted to tell Ben about my trip, but there were several others at the table. Before I left, he said, "Why don't you come out for coffee next Saturday morning, Lynne? We haven' had a chance to really talk for quite awhile."

"I'd like that," I said. "It's a date."

CHAPTER 22

INAH RETURNED FROM Kurt's that Sunday for dinner but had to work at the pool in the afternoon. We had tacos on the porch for lunch. I told her about Ben's invitation for the following Saturday.

"I plan to talk to them about the trailer. I really think it should be destroyed."

She looked out at the trailer in the back yard. "Somehow it seems sacrilegious or something."

I smiled. "Not exactly, but I know what you mean. We'll see what Ben and Minnie say, but I definitely don't want it here. I'm thinking about looking at a new one. They're making reproductions of the old 'canned hams,' they called them."

"What's a canned ham? And you mean you still want to camp?"

I explained canned hams and then said, "I really enjoyed the group of women I met on that trip, and even though I'm not outdoorsy, they have a variety of activities. A lot of them have been through some pretty rough times." I told her about Teri's son and Victoria's cancer.

She got up and picked up her plate. "Well, gotta go to work, Mom. Someone in this family needs to keep a regular job." She grinned and kissed me.

"And we appreciate your supporting us." I whacked her behind as she headed for the kitchen.

I WAS STARTING some laundry a little later when Kurt called. We had spoken so little lately that I panicked.

"Is something wrong?" I said, my heart pounding. "Is Dinah alright?"

He sounded puzzled. "Isn't she working?"

"As far as I know." I took a deep breath. "I didn't expect you to be calling and thought—"

"Relax," he said, almost sarcastically. "*You're* the one with the high-risk life style."

I bristled. "So you only called to mock?"

His voice softened. "No, but I think we need to talk about our situation. Can I come over for a little bit?"

So, maybe that apology was coming. But I didn't appreciate his cold shoulder the last couple of weeks.

"I'm kind of busy right now. How about in an hour or so?"

"Great. I'll see you then."

I went about my tasks with a lighter heart. Kurt and I had started out, like most couples, madly in love, and that only seemed to grow when Dinah was born. But the added stress of her approaching teens and several job changes for both of us took the bloom off the rose, and we had been struggling.

After Dinah disappeared the summer before, we had entered counseling and — I thought — made good progress. But the change in the timeline brought about by my trip had upset all of that. Maybe we could get things turned around again.

When Kurt arrived, I poured us each a glass of iced tea and we headed, of course, for the porch. It had always been our living room, dining room, office, and occasionally bedroom on nice summer days.

Kurt looked around at this pleasant refuge, rather wistfully, and told me about his and Dinah's weekend. On Saturday, they had actually gone roller-skating at a nearby town that still had a rink. I couldn't imagine Kurt on skates or putting himself in any position where he might embarrass himself. He laughed self-consciously about his performance.

He cleared his throat. "Lynne, I don't think this counseling is going anywhere. I think we have to admit that our marriage is dead and we need to move on." He made designs in the condensation on his glass with his finger.

I sat stunned. A rock fell in my stomach and I just looked at him.

"Maybe it would be best if we started seeing other people. We need to stop raising Dinah's hopes that we're going to get back together." He didn't look at me, only continued to draw patterns on his glass.

"I—I thought the counseling was going well."

"Well, I did too but then that stunt you pulled—"

"Kurt!" I slammed my hand down on the table, making the ice tremble in the glasses. "I *explained* what happened. I was trying to *help* someone."

"Maybe that's what you thought—"

"Do you have someone in mind?"

"What? What are you talking about?"

"Your comment about seeing other people. Are you already looking?"

"Well...no." But his hesitation was the last straw.

"Please leave."

"If you can't talk about this sensibly..."

I couldn't control the tears—something I do if I'm angry as much as if I'm sad. "I thought you were coming over here to apologize. And then you throw this at me. Obviously I was way off base." I stood up. "Please leave."

He got up, too. "We need to plan how to tell Dinah..."

"*You* tell her. This is your idea." I thought back to her recent comment about how sure she was that her dad would come around to forgiving me. I wasn't so sure I had done anything that needed to be forgiven.

"Fine." His tone said it wasn't, but he walked to the door. "I'll call you after *I've* taken care of it."

I slammed the door behind him.

I SPENT THE REST of the afternoon picking things up and putting them down, getting things out and putting them away.

What had happened? I was at a loss as to where things went wrong. Well, I knew the trigger—my trip in the trailer. But something else had to be behind this. In the timeline that I remembered, Kurt had become more relaxed and amiable in the last year. He had started his own business developing software apps and had seemed so much happier.

This—this was the old Kurt that had caused our separation in the first place. I wasn't so blind as to think I hadn't contributed to that break. One could say we didn't play well together.

I managed to pull myself together before Dinah came home. I was determined that Kurt should explain the 'seeing other people' to her. When I thought about that, I wondered if he really did have his eye on someone else. Someone he had known from work, perhaps. Kurt was not a social animal. I couldn't imagine him picking up a woman in a bar. I shook my head as if it would help my brain and searched for something else to focus on.

The upcoming Sisters on the Fly 'Junk Jaunt' event came to mind. Just the thing to take my mind off Kurt. With perfect timing, my phone rang.

"Lynne?" I didn't quite recognize the voice. "You may not remember me. This is Teri Crowley from Sisters on the Fly. We met about ten years ago at Paulie's Shoots?"

Of course, she didn't realize that for me, that was only two weeks ago. "Yes, Teri—of course I remember you. How have you been?"

"Fine, fine. I saw that you finally became a member of Sisters. What took you so long?"

"Um, I don't know. Life kind of gets in the way, you know."

"I do know. Well, glad you're joining us! I'm one of the 'Wranglers' for this region so I'll be sending you a welcome letter."

"It's so weird that you would call right now." I laughed. "I was just thinking about the Junk Jaunt coming up in a month or so."

Teri actually squealed. "That would be great! I'm going and Victoria is, too. I'm trying to talk Glynis into it. And Joan—did you meet her?"

"I don't think so. I don't remember her."

"You'll love her. So do you still have your old trailer?"

"Nooo—I had to get rid of it several years ago," I lied.

"I'm thinking of getting one of those new retro reproductions."

"Well, if you don't have one by then, stay with me. I'm so excited. I can't wait to tell the others."

I wanted to ask about Melanie and Bev but decided that could wait. Maybe they would be there.

"How is your son doing?"

"Wow, let's see — he's been in a group home now for about four years and loves it. He comes to stay with me occasionally but can't wait to get back with his buddies. It's a relief not to worry about him so much."

We chatted a little more and then hung up. Her call seemed like a safety net, catching me right before I hit bottom and providing just the support and distraction I needed to get through this with Kurt.

I went on line to check out retro campers.

I WAITED SEVERAL days until I could cool down from Kurt's bombshell and then tried to call him at home. Dinah was getting braces and we had to work out how we were paying for them. There was no answer. I left a message but didn't hear back all afternoon. He finally called back while I was fixing supper, and by that time I was annoyed again.

"Lynne?" he said.

"It's about time. I thought you had some big project you were working on. Not too busy to take the afternoon off, I guess" I didn't know where this was coming from, except that everything he did irritated me now.

"What? I just got home. You know I don't get off work until 5:00."

"Get off? You're back working at CBT? Or somewhere else?"

"What are you talking about? I never left there."

"But you started your own business and were working at home."

"You have been lost in a fantasy world ever since you got back from that trip. I'd love to go on my own but I never did."

"By the way, have you talked to Dinah about our situation?"

"No, I've been waiting for the right time."

Kurt did not like unpleasant tasks. Well, that was fine by me—I wasn't in any rush. I paused and calmed down. "Kurt, who were we going to for counseling?"

I knew he was shaking his head and his voice was exasperated. "Lori Masters. One of your friends recommended her."

"Not Scott Waghorn?"

"No, Lori Masters."

This might explain a lot, but I needed to think about it. I made my voice more business-like. "The reason I called is that I got the estimate for Dinah's braces. We need to figure out how we are going to pay for them."

His patience was gone. "Lynne, I have dental insurance and a flex-spending account at work that will pay for it. This shouldn't be a surprise to you."

"Oh." Maybe it shouldn't be a surprise but it was. I didn't know he was still working for someone else.

"Okay, thanks." I hung up before he could add mental incompetency to my list of parental deficiencies.

LORI MASTERS, NOT Scott Waghorn. I didn't know anything about Lori Masters but obviously when the timeline changed, some tiny glitch had caused us to go to her instead of Scott. I thought maybe they were in the same office.

Lori had not encouraged Kurt to start his own business like Scott had and he was still an unhappy worker bee. I filed this information in the 'Save the Marriage' slot in my brain, and turned to the 'Get Rid of the Trailer' slot.

I wanted to be prepared for my visit with Ben and Minnie on Saturday. When I bought it from Ben originally, I thought that if I didn't camp in it, I could make it an office or guest house. The guest house thing was definitely out and I had very few out of town guests anyway. I wasn't comfortable with even using it during the day as an office any more. It couldn't be sold either, for obvious reasons. It seemed that the only reasonable alternative was to destroy it.

On Friday night at supper, Dinah said "Are you still going to talk to Ben and Minnie tomorrow about the camper?"

"Yes, I am. Why?"

"Can I go along? I haven't seen them in quite a while and I'd like to hear what you decide."

I thought about it a moment. Dinah was well aware of what the camper could do from the previous summer and I supposed she had as much of a stake in its future as I did.

"Sure. About 10:00. You'll have to get up early." I grinned at her.

She stuck out her tongue and got up to take her dishes to the kitchen, her phone already in her other hand.

THE NEXT MORNING as we drove into the driveway of Ben's farm, the sky hung low and gray. But their cheerful kitchen was welcoming and smelled of rich coffee and cinnamon.

Minnie had set the round table with bright Fiesta ware and a golden brown coffee cake held the center of the table.

"Dinah, do you drink coffee?" Minnie asked.

"Yes, please."

"She uses a *lot* of milk and sugar," I added.

We seated ourselves and Ben questioned Dinah about school while Minnie served us generous slices of cake.

Ben turned to me. "Have you done any camping lately?"

I realized then that Ben and Minnie would have been part of the new timeline also and wouldn't remember our conversation about saving Naomi Burks' friend. I began at the beginning, explaining first that the trip had caused a changed timeline and that I had told them about it beforehand.

Unlike Kurt and Dinah, neither of them doubted my story. When I finished, I said to Ben, "What happened here, Ben? If I went back and changed events so that Melanie never changed her name and moved here, why wasn't I here that weekend? Why did I even go? And why do I remember the previous string of events and you don't?"

Ben shrugged. "I can't answer that. Maybe traveling in the trailer gives you that ability. Maybe time travel causes a glitch in the continuum that things slip through—I don't know."

Dinah sat there nodding. "This comes up in a lot of the time travel books."

We hadn't talked about this before. "So what's the answer?"

"Nobody knows," she said with a little grin.

I looked at Ben again. "I remember the last ten years as they were originally; I have no memory of, for example, the last three months without Naomi Burks in them. In other words, Dinah may not have the same memories of the last decade as I do."

I hadn't considered any of these things before. What if I had been a part of my daughter's life without remembering anything from ages five to fifteen? A kind of despair washed over me. Even if I wanted to go back next year and 'put things back,' I couldn't—not exactly.

Ben said, "Maybe the only differences between the two versions is the appearance of Naomi Burks and her interaction with you."

I shook my head. "I might have thought so but I found out Kurt still works for CBT and that we have been seeing a different counselor than I remember. In my version, we went to Scott Waghorn and he encouraged Kurt to start his own business, which was going very well, by the way. Why would those things change? And how many other things are different?"

"You'll drive yourself crazy trying to figure that out. You'd have to compare memories item by item with someone for the whole ten years," Ben said.

Minnie leaned over and patted my hand and spoke in her soft voice. "You did a good thing."

"I hope so. Anyway, what I came here to talk to you about is what to do with the trailer. I'm convinced I should never use it again and I certainly can't sell it. I wonder—I don't want to hurt your feelings—if it should be burned." I looked from him to Minnie.

They both looked shocked. I tried to explain myself further. "I mean, I've learned that so many things can go wrong unintentionally…"

Minnie patted my hand again. "Let us think on it. Meanwhile, would you feel better if it was back out here?"

"I would. I don't know why, but I would."

"What about a museum?" Dinah said.

"A museum." Ben rubbed his chin. "An RV Museum, you mean? Not a bad idea."

"It would have to be inside," Dinah went on, "someplace where it would be locked up at night."

"Honey, I think you might be on to something," I said.

She tossed her hair and put her chin in the air. "I'm not dumb just because I'm blond." We all laughed.

I decided to go back to town, hitch up the trailer, and bring it back out that very afternoon. I was that anxious to get rid of it.

CHAPTER 23

W E RETURNED THE TRAILER to the space behind Ben's barn. I secretly hoped that the weeds would surround it and swallow it up. I was becoming very resentful, and yet frightened of this heretofore cute piece of Americana.

Dinah planned to show Ben how to do a search on the Internet for RV Museums. Together they hoped to find some possibilities.

Meanwhile, I made arrangements with Kurt to meet the next week on an evening when Dinah was busy. I wanted to really talk this out. If he was determined our marriage was done for, there was nothing I could do. But I wanted to try and bring back the benefits of the timeline I remembered.

We decided on a neutral ground at a local sports bar — private enough spots and enough noise that we should be able to have a conversation without being overheard. I took a little more care with my appearance than I had been inclined to of late, smiling to myself as I wondered what Kurt's reaction would be if I showed up in one of the outfits favored by the Sisters on the Fly.

He was already in a booth when I got there. He glanced up, barely interested, when I sat down and said, "I ordered you a white wine."

"Thank you." I smiled with effort, gritting my teeth at his efforts to keep control.

We looked at the menu and ordered our suppers, making small talk about Dinah's job and dental work. After the food arrived, I said "You're probably wondering why I called this meeting," and smiled at the feeble joke.

He cocked his head, did *not* smile, and said, "Yes."

"First, when I tried to call you last week during the day, I was surprised you weren't there because in my 'other life' (I threw in air quotes for good measure), we were going through counseling with Scott Waghorn, not Lori Masters. And he encouraged you to quit your job and start a freelance business. You were really excited this spring about an app you were developing to help elderly people with dementia."

He looked interested, but still skeptical. "Frankly, I find this whole 'other life' thing pretty preposterous."

"Don't you think I do? If I was on *any* kind of medication, I'd think I was hallucinating. I just joined the group, Sisters on the Fly, who sponsored the event I went to two weeks ago—although actually it was ten years ago. I got a call from one of the women I met there and she said 'I met you ten years ago.' I *believe* it all happened. You experienced time travel last summer—how is the 'other life' thing—a changed timeline, any more preposterous than that?"

He shrugged but didn't say anything so I continued. "That's not what I wanted to talk to you about. I have seen how much difference it made for you—and for us—when you quit your job and started your own business. Would you be willing to give it another try and see Scott Waghorn?"

He didn't answer so I took a deep breath and continued. "I'm getting rid of the camper. I talked to Ben and Minnie about it last weekend. My plan was to burn it but Dinah suggested donating it to an RV museum and we think that would work. I've already taken it to Ben's. I'm done with it."

"I wish you wouldn't involve Dinah..."

"I *know*, Kurt, but Dinah's been involved in this since the beginning and it was her wish. I wouldn't have included her if I thought there was any way it would harm her."

He shook his head. "I don't know..."

"Please think about it. Even if our marriage is beyond

saving—and I don't agree that it is—, I want you to be happy. Believe me, you were a different person when you went on your own. Will you think about talking to Scott?"

"I'll think about it. That's all I can promise."

I relaxed. I didn't want to push it any farther at this point. We tackled our food and I told him more about the Sisters and some of the women I had met.

He even smiled at my description of Victoria's camper and the cowgirl prom. "Sounds like they have a good time."

"Their motto is 'We have more fun than anyone.' I think I will plan on going to the Junk Jaunt event in a few weeks. Teri—the woman who called—said I could stay with her in her camper."

He didn't comment any further. We finished our lunches and paid the bill. When we got out on the sidewalk, he gave me a tentative hug and said simply, "We'll see what happens."

I CONTINUED MAKING my plans for the Junk Jaunt. Meanwhile, I looked into dude ranches that still had vacancies in August and brought brochures home for Dinah to look at. Dinah was excited about it and we spent several evenings weighing the pros and cons of each. I had to caution her not to put too much emphasis on the cute cowboys in the pictures. We made a decision and I got reservations for a week.

I called Teri Crowley back and told her I would take her up on her offer of a bed in her camper. We discussed snacks and meals, dividing up the responsibilities.

I talked to Kurt off and on, mostly about Dinah. He never mentioned our conversation. Finally, a few days before I left for the Junk Jaunt, I screwed up my courage to ask.

"Have you thought more about talking to Scott?"

"I've thought about it."

"And—?"

"I don't know yet, Lynne. I don't like being pushed."

Sorree, I wanted to say, that's exactly why you should get out of that job. Instead, I said, "I care, Kurt. I'm not trying to push." Of course, I was.

"Have a nice time this weekend," he said.

THE CAMPGROUND WHERE the sisters gathered for the Junk Jaunt was older but sites were very spacious. Even though it was midsummer and rain had been scarce, I was glad to see it sat on a ridge, and the lake and river were a hefty downward hike. We should stay relatively dry, whatever the weather.

I pulled into the site number Teri had given me. She hadn't arrived yet so I got out to walk around. I was really looking forward to this. No self-assigned rescue missions or impending weather disasters to think about. At least that I knew of.

A few sites down, there was an old camper of the canned ham type that had been painted with flowers, animals, trees, and cartoon children. A bright flowered outdoor rug covered the ground in front of the camper and a multi-colored awning shaded the area. A woman lounged in an aluminum and webbing rocker, reading.

I walked up to her. "Hi," I said. "Are you with the Sisters on the Fly?"

She put down her book and smiled. "Yes, I am. Joan Barker." She held out her hand. "And you are?"

"Lynne McBriar. I think Teri Crowley mentioned you. I'm going to bunk with her this weekend. I don't have a camper of my own right now."

"As far as I know, I'm the only one here — besides you. Have a chair." She indicated another folding chair leaning against the camper.

We spent a pleasant hour discussing her camper and events she had taken part in. Her aunt was a painter who had done the outside decorating on her trailer.

Several others arrived, including Glynis and Glorie, and some that I didn't know. I was beginning to wonder what had happened to Teri, when she called.

"Omigod. I am about an hour away. I had a flat tire and had to get it fixed, so don't give up on me!"

"Wow, that's a shame! Of course we wouldn't give up on you!"

"Trouble is, I have the hamburgers for tonight's supper. Is Glynis there?"

"Sure. Do you want to talk to her?"

"No, just tell her the deal and maybe she can get a fire started so we can cook when I get there."

"No problem. Take care."

I found Glynis and explained Teri's tardiness. She took charge and got a couple of women hauling firewood to Teri's site. By the time Teri arrived, we had a good blaze going. Victoria, Patsy, and Sandy were there too. I didn't see Bev or Melanie but in the bustle helping Teri set up and getting ready for supper, there was no chance to ask about them.

Supper was a traditional American menu: hamburgers, Glorie's potato salad, a big cast iron Dutch oven of baked beans, and sliced homegrown tomatoes. Sweet corn roasted over another fire. We dragged a couple of picnic tables over from other sites and covered them with a variety of outdoor tablecloths.

Discussion at supper centered on the Junk Jaunt the next day. Patsy produced copies of maps showing sales going on in five surrounding small towns and along the roads in between. Glorie was not drinking and I wondered if she had quit. Contrary to her comment on the river years ago, she seemed to be having as much fun as the rest and certainly was as entertaining. The evening of laughter and ribbing ended with a variation on S'mores—saltines with a caramel and a marshmallow.

BY THE TIME Teri and I got inside to make up our

beds, we were both ready to collapse.

"Tomorrow sounds like fun, although I'm not sure I need any more junk," I said.

"It's the looking that's fun," Teri said.

"Do you ever hear anything from Melanie or Bev?"

Teri sat down on the edge of her bed and took a long draw from her water bottle. "Not much. Melanie is still a member but Bev is in prison."

"What? Why?"

"Bev was supplying pain killers to Justin, Melanie's son. He eventually moved on to heroin and went through lots more rehab. I think he's clean now, but he had a rough time."

I realized my mouth was hanging open and closed it to process this.

"Bev—?" I couldn't finish.

"I think when it started, she was trying to help. The kid had an injury that caused him a lot of pain and when his doctor cut off his painkillers, Bev stepped in. She worked for a pharmaceutical company if you remember."

"Yeah, but…Melanie didn't know she was doing that?"

"Not a clue. Her husband suspected it. That's why he didn't want Melanie hanging around with Bev. Justin even attacked his mother once when he was high and his dad was out of town, but she wouldn't press charges."

I was stunned. I remembered reading about the assault that I thought Tabor was guilty of. "Did anyone else know this at the time?"

She shook her head and took another drink of water. "Nope. Melanie and Bev grew up together and Mel wouldn't believe anything bad about Bev. Bev never charged Justin for the painkillers but apparently because of her financial problems after she lost her job, when Justin sent his friends to her, she started dealing."

"Oh, Lord." I leaned back against the wall and my head whirled. So by saving Bev's life and hence Melanie from trying to throw her own life away, I had created *this* chaos.

Finally I said, "So when we were at Paulie's Shoots, those attacks on Bev..."

Teri got up and put the water bottle in a recycling bag and leaned against the counter. "No one ever figured out the whole story. They think the falling rock was just that. And that she fabricated the snake story. The shots might have been real—whether the drug company really was after her or the parent of some other kid she was dealing to, it's hard to say. Remember the girl at the kayak rental place described someone with a tattoo who asked for information about where the group would be getting off the river. You never heard any of this on the news?"

I shook my head. I had been in a different timeline but that was a little hard to explain. "Wow. I had no idea. So how is Melanie?"

"She doesn't come to very many events, and when she does, she's pretty quiet. She doesn't let anyone get too close — emotionally, I mean — and I don't know if she will ever trust anyone again. It's a pretty sad story. And on that note, I think I'd better get to bed."

"Me too. Thanks for putting me up this weekend."

I didn't get to sleep for a long time.

Chapter

24

THE WEEKEND WAS a resounding success, and, other than the shocking news Teri had imparted, I had a great time. The weather held and we trekked around the county gravel roads on Saturday, marveling at the variety of items for sale and at things now being sold for $20 that we had thrown out years before. I bought a crocheted tablecloth with only a couple of holes to use on my porch and the others found equally delightful purchases.

I had come prepared this time with a little cowboy finery of my own and so was ready for the Saturday night festivities. There was no band, but roasted chicken and jambalaya filled us up. By the time I left Sunday morning, I had made several new friends and plans to attend other events.

On the drive home, my thoughts returned to Melanie and Bev and how I had affected their lives. I would never know all of the effects my actions created or how the timeline change caused things such as Kurt and me seeing a different counselor. I now believed that the trips that Dinah, Kurt, and I had taken the summer before had probably caused changes too. I was convinced that I never wanted to time travel again and was more determined than ever to get rid of the trailer.

WHEN DINAH CAME BACK from Kurt's that Sunday evening, she asked how my weekend was.

"It was great. I reconnected with some of the women from the Missouri trip although they had sure aged a lot in the past few weeks. They looked ten years older!"

Dinah looked at me, a little surprised because I had always lectured her on not criticizing others' looks. Then a slow smile came over her face. "Oh. I get it. What about the woman whose life you saved?"

I sighed. "That news isn't so good." I told her what Teri had told me.

"She got her best friend's son hooked on drugs?"

"It appears so—or at least she certainly helped. And several other kids."

"Oh, Mom. You should have let her die."

"That's a little harsh. I don't know that any other lives were lost. But it certainly has sold me on sticking to present-time travel."

Dinah nodded. I could tell she was churning this all through her mind. "Ben and I need to find a place for that camper."

"How about if we have Ben and Minnie to supper sometime this week and we can work on that."

"Great idea! Can I call them? We could have spaghetti." Dinah's favorite and perpetual request.

"We can talk about the menu later. Yes, go ahead and call. I'm free every night this week so it depends on what nights you have to work."

"I only work Tuesday night this week. Where's their number?" She had her phone out ready to go.

"In the phone book."

She rolled her eyes at me and went to look it up.

"Hi Ben," I heard her say. "It's me, Dinah. What are you guys doing this week?'

A long pause while I'm sure Ben explained that it would be easier to answer her question if she would be more specific. After a lot of back and forth, they settled on Wednesday night.

We compromised on a spaghetti pasta salad with tomatoes, olives, pepperoni and ham, since the weather was quite warm. Dinah didn't have to work Wednesday so she wheedled my mother into helping her make rolls. When I got home from work, she had also set the table with my best china and cloth napkins folded like swans.

"Wow!" I said. "Pretty fancy. Where'd you learn to fold napkins like that?"

"I looked it up on the 'Net.'"

I gave her a hug. "Aren't you the cleverest thing!" And it ran through my mind how close I had come to not sharing her life because of the trailer several times. Tears gathered in my eyes.

"Don't cry, Mom. I won't do it again." She grinned.

"No, thinking about how I've almost lost you several times because of that camper. We've *got* to get rid of it."

"We will." She patted me on the shoulder. "We'll come up with something tonight."

I wiped my eyes and headed to the kitchen. "Okay. Time to cook. You can chop up the pepperoni and ham."

WHEN BEN AND MINNIE arrived, there were hugs all around, and we moved out to the porch. Ben had a glass of red wine and Minnie asked for coffee. We had put Dinah's rolls in the warming oven, and sat down to wait.

"So tell us about your weekend with the Sisters on the Fly," Ben said, giving the name a bit of a flourish.

"It was great. First I have to tell you what I learned about Melanie and Bev." I repeated the information that Teri had given me.

"Oh, that poor woman!" Minnie said. "She can't catch a break, can she?"

"It would seem not," I said. "I am more convinced than ever that we have to somehow 'neutralize' that camper. We can talk about it over supper. Dinah, would you help me get the food?"

Soon we were passing rolls and the bowl of pasta, plus some of my mother's pickled beets. I told them about the rest of the weekend and some of the events scheduled in the future.

Minnie's eyes were shining. "It sounds like so much fun, Lynne. I wish they had something like that when I was younger!"

"No reason why you can't go with me sometime," I said. "Now that I've become so proficient in pulling and backing up a trailer—" at this Dinah cleared her throat and rolled her eyes—"I'm looking at one of the new retro trailers. Seriously, Minnie, you would love this group and they would love you."

Ben pushed his pasta around his plate a little bit with his fork and then laid it down on his plate and clasped his hands under his chin. "Meanwhile, you are right, Lynne, we need to get rid of the old camper. Our concern, when you suggested burning it, was that it might somehow change some of events as they are now. We have no idea, of course, but we don't want to take a chance."

"Right," I said. "I don't want to take that chance either."

"So a museum would be the best choice," Dinah insisted.

"Have you looked for any, my dear?" Ben asked her.

"Yup," Dinah said. "I'll show you after supper. There's several. There's a big one in Indiana—"

"In Elkhart," Ben supplied.

"Yeah, and a couple in California and one in Illinois. I can't remember where else."

"Illinois — that would be great," I said, "if we could find one that close." After supper Minnie and I cleared the dishes while Ben and Dinah huddled over her laptop. When we returned from the kitchen, Ben sat up. "I'm going to call this place in Illinois tomorrow. It's small and part of an RV dealership."

THE NEXT NIGHT when I got home from the office, Ben called with excitement in his voice.

"I talked to that dealer, Lynne, and they would be thrilled to have the camper."

"Can we put some kind of stipulation that they can't ever sell it?" I asked.

"Hmmm. I see what you're thinking. I doubt if we could do that if we give them the title. Have to talk to a lawyer."

"What if we loaned it to them? You know, in art museums a lot of times it says 'On loan from blah blah blah.'"

"That's an idea. I'll check it out. But you know that means you could get it back sometime. The title's in your name."

"Well, I'll deal with that then. I don't know what else to do. We can't tell anyone what it can do — well, we can but no one will believe us without a demonstration and I don't want to do that. And I don't want to be responsible if they sell it to someone who would try and use it."

"Then it sounds like a loan would be the best idea."

IT WAS TWO DAYS before I heard back from Ben.

"We're all set," he said. "I told the dealer that you wanted to put it in the museum on loan. By the way, he thinks I'm your father." He chuckled. "He'll make a space for it and you can take it over any time that's convenient."

We discussed plans to take it over on the next Saturday and I had just hung up when Kurt called. I hadn't talked to him since before the weekend when he told me not to push him.

"How did your trip go?"

"Fine. It was a lot of fun. But Teri—the woman I stayed with—told me some disturbing news about Melanie." I repeated the story for the third time.

"You aren't—I mean, I hope you're not thinking of going back and trying to change things again." He was more worried than forceful.

"Absolutely not. I've learned my lesson. I heard from Ben right before you called. He's arranged for an RV museum in Illinois to take it." I explained about his concern of what might happen if we destroyed it.

"So you're selling it to them or just giving it to them?"

"Neither. It will be a loan."

"Lynne—"

"Hear me out. We are afraid if they have the title, they could at some point sell it to someone and it could get used again. We don't want to take that chance."

"I see. Okay." He sounded unsure but accepting.

"We're going to take it over next Saturday morning. Do you want to go along?"

"Oh! Well, yeah, I could ride along. Is Dinah going?"

"Definitely. She did the research to find this place."

"I think I would like to go."

DURING THE NEXT WEEK, I probably felt more relaxed than I had since Naomi Burks had walked into my office. It was a relief to accept that I couldn't change the past without huge repercussions and even more of a relief that the camper would be in a secure place. On Saturday, we picked Kurt up in the morning and headed out to Ben's farm.

Dinah and I hooked the camper up to the Jeep while Kurt watched with a kind of surprised respect.

Minnie clutched Ben's arm while they looked on too and I realized how afraid they were that if something happened to the camper, Minnie might be whisked away from Ben. I would be glad to get this done.

I drove and Kurt navigated. Ben had written down instructions from the dealer. He and Minnie opted not to go along. I suspected that they were afraid of an accident or something—kind of a superstition.

We found the dealer without any problem. The museum was in a steel building behind the dealership. The owner was busy so we looked around in awe at the age of some of the campers and camping paraphernalia — coolers, lanterns, cookstoves, and so forth.

Dinah called us from one to another with "Mom, check this one out!" and "Dad, look at this one!"

"Ms. McBriar?" A tall, graying man had come up behind me and held out his hand. "I'm Herb Branson. I saw your camper out in the lot — what a unique item!"

You have no idea, I thought, but smiled and said "Thank you. This is my husband, Kurt, and my daughter, Dinah."

He clasped his hands behind his back. "May I ask, why did you decide to get rid of it?"

I had prepared for this question. "I'm worried about preserving it. And it's not as convenient as the new ones. But I think people would enjoy seeing it and you have some wonderful specimens here."

I saw his eyes light up at my words 'new ones'. "Thank you for saying that. So are you thinking of a new one? We can help with that, too."

"I would like to look before we leave. Right now, I want to take care of mine first."

"Of course. Why don't you come back to my office. We have had a loan agreement drawn up and I'll need to see the title and make a copy of that. Meanwhile, is it okay if one of my guys pull it in to one of our work areas and unhook it?"

"Sure." I handed him the keys to the Jeep.

"Dirk!" He called a man over and handed him the keys with instructions of where to park it. We then followed Herb to his office and took seats in the visitors chairs. It seemed like it took more paperwork to loan somebody something than to buy a car or a house. Finally we finished and he ushered us out to a neighboring building where Dirk had parked the camper.

Herb Branson took the keys and unlocked the door. He entered it with a look of awe as if he was entering an ancient Greek ruin. He turned and spoke out the door.

"Have you remodeled this at all?"

I told him what I had done to remove later remodeling, taking it back to the original. "I refinished the wood because it had been painted over, but that is the original floor."

"Okay, we need to document all of that for our visitors." He bounced down the steps and rubbed his hands together. "Thank you so much. We'll take good care of it."

"Herb, will you call the office?" came a disembodied voice over a loudspeaker.

"Oh, excuse me, I'll be right back." He took off at a jog.

"Can I go in it one more time?" Dinah said.

I nodded. "Sure. Just don't fall asleep."

She grinned. "Don't worry."

While we waited, Kurt's phone rang. "Yes? Oh,

Thanks for returning my call…Okay. Next Wednesday? Thanks."

He put his phone away. I looked at him. "Everything okay?"

"I hope so." He smiled. "That was Scott Waghorn."

I took his hand, squeezed it and smiled too.

Thank You

For taking your time to share the time travel trailer's adventures. Just as the sound of a tree falling in the forest depends on hearers, a book only matters if it has readers. Please consider sharing your thoughts with other readers in a review on Amazon or emailing me at karen.musser.nortman@gmail.com. My website at www.karenmussernortman.com provides updates on my books, my blog, and photos of our for-real camping trips.

You can get a free copy of the second Frannie Shoemaker Campground Mystery, *THE BLUE COYOTE,* if you sign up for my Favorite Readers email list to receive occasional notices about my new books and special offers.

Go to this link:
www.karenmussernortman.com

Acknowledgments

The idea for this book was suggested by Dee Ann Hess, a Sister on the Fly. She also agreed to be a beta reader, especially to vet the kayaking segment. I also want to thank my other readers, Ginge, Marcia, Marian, and Elaine.

Paulie's Shoots is very loosely based on Johnson's Shut-ins in Missouri, a wonderful state park with a new campground. The old one was destroyed by a flash flood in December, 2005 when the Tam Sauk Reservoir breached. But flash flooding from torrential rains is occasionally a problem in campgrounds across the country.

Other Books by the Author

The Time Travel Trailer: (A Chanticleer 2015 Paranormal category winner) A 1937 vintage camper trailer half hidden in weeds catches Lynne McBriar's eye when she is visiting an elderly friend Ben. Ben eagerly sells it to her and she just as eagerly embarks on a restoration. But after each remodel, sleeping in the trailer lands Lynne and her daughter Dinah in a previous decade—exciting, yet frightening. Glimpses of their home town and ancestors fifty or sixty years earlier is exciting and also offers some clues to the mystery of Ben's lost love. But when Dinah makes a trip on her own, she separates herself from her mother by decades. It is a trip that may upset the future if Lynne and her estranged husband can't team up to bring their daughter back.

The award-winning Frannie Shoemaker Campground Mysteries:
Bats and Bones: (An IndieBRAG Medallion honoree) Frannie and Larry Shoemaker are retirees who enjoy weekend camping with their friends in state parks. They anticipate the usual hiking, campfires, good food, and interesting side trips among the bluffs of beautiful Bat Cave State Park until a dead body turns up. Confined in the campground and surrounded by strangers, Frannie is drawn into the investigation.

The Blue Coyote: (An IndieBRAG Medallion honoree and a 2013 Chanticleer CLUE finalist) Frannie and Larry Shoemaker love taking their grandchildren, Sabet and Joe, camping with them. But at Bluffs State Park, Frannie finds herself worrying more than usual about their safety, and when another young girl disappears from the campground in broad daylight, her fears increase. Accusations against Larry and her add to the cloud over their heads.

Peete and Repeat: (An IndieBRAG Medallion honoree, 2013 Chanticleer CLUE finalist, and 2014 Chanticleer Mystery and Mayhem finalist) A biking and camping trip to southeastern Minnesota turns into double trouble for Frannie Shoemaker and her friends as she deals with a canoeing mishap and a couple of bodies.

The Lady of the Lake: (An IndieBRAG Medallion honoree, 2014 Chanticleer CLUE finalist) A trip down memory lane is fine if you don't stumble on a body. Frannie Shoemaker and her friends camp at Old Dam Trail State Park near one of Donna Nowak's childhood homes and take in the county fair. But the present intrudes when a body surfaces. Donna becomes the focus of the investigation and Frannie wonders if the police shouldn't be looking closer at the victim's many enemies.

To Cache a Killer: Geocaching isn't supposed to be about finding dead bodies. But when retiree, Frannie

Shoemaker go camping, standard definitions don't apply. A weekend in a beautiful state park in Iowa buzzes with fund-raising events, a search for Ninja turtles, a bevy of suspects, and lots of great food. But are the campers in the wrong place at the wrong time once too often?

A Campy Christmas: A Holiday novella. The Shoemakers and Ferraros plan to spend Christmas in Texas and then take a camping trip through the Southwest. But those plans are stopped cold when they hit a rogue ice storm in Missouri and they end up snowbound in a campground. And that's just the beginning. Includes recipes and winter camping tips.

Happy Camper Tips and Recipes: All of the tips and recipes from the first four Frannie Shoemaker books in one convenient paperback or Kindle version that you can keep in your camping supplies!

ABOUT THE AUTHOR

Karen Musser Nortman is the author of the Frannie Shoemaker Campground cozy mystery series, including the BRAGMedallion honoree, Bats and Bones. After previous incarnations as a secondary social studies teacher (22 years) and a test developer (18 years), she returned to her childhood dream of writing a novel.

Karen and her husband Butch originally tent camped when their children were young and switched to a travel trailer when sleeping on the ground lost its romantic adventure. They take frequent weekend jaunts with friends to parks in Iowa and surrounding states, plus occasional longer trips. Entertainment on these trips has ranged from geocaching and hiking/biking to barbecue contests, balloon fests, and buck skinners' rendezvous. Out of these trips came the Frannie Shoemaker Campground Mysteries and now *The Time Travel Trailer*.

More information is available on her website at www.karenmussernortman.com.

Made in the USA
San Bernardino, CA
16 August 2017